DRIVEN TO DEATH

"You know what I think?" Bobby said, and leant back against the window. "I think there was someone there with her. Someone, the man she was involved with, was fed up with her, wanted her to leave him alone. I think he knew she wasn't going to give him up that easy. He put the sleeping tablets into the wine and then when she was asleep he wiped his prints off the bottle and placed her fingers back on it."

"Bobby, this is a bit far-fetched."

"He took the container of the tablets away in his pocket and put the note onto the dashboard and left her there to die. He knew that the police would accept the whole thing at face value."

He stopped and put his head against the window pane. Jessie lifted her arm and touched his shoulder.

"And we're not the only ones; someone else knows . . ."

POINT CRIME

DRIVEN TO DEATH

Anne Cassidy

Cover illustration by David Wyatt

SCHOLASTIC

Scholastic Children's Books,
Scholastic Publications Ltd,
7–9 Pratt Street, London NW1 0AE, UK

Scholastic Inc.,
555 Broadway, New York, NY 10012-3999, USA

Scholastic Canada Ltd,
123 Newkirk Road, Richmond Hill,
Ontario, Canada L4C 3G5

Ashton Scholastic Pty Ltd,
P O Box 579, Gosford, New South Wales,
Australia

Ashton Scholastic Ltd,
Private Bag 92801, Penrose, Auckland,
New Zealand

First published by Scholastic Publications Ltd, 1994

Text copyright © Anne Cassidy, 1994

Cover artwork copyright © David Wyatt, 1994

ISBN 0 590 55429 8

Typeset by TW Typesetting, Midsomer Norton, Avon
Printed by Cox & Wyman Ltd, Reading, Berks

For my sister Sam

1

Tuesday 6th October.

It was exactly a year since Laurie had died.

Jessie was sitting on her bed. To her side was a patterned box that was full of photographs and she had one of them in her hand.

She got up and looked out of her bedroom window. The sky was the colour of cement and the clouds were so low that they seemed to be resting on the rooftops of the houses opposite.

The photograph had been taken some months before the suicide. Jessie turned it over. On the back, in Laurie's handwriting, were the words, *Happy days. Love, Laurie*.

It was a picture of the college tutor group that she and Laurie had been in. There were about a dozen of them, all crushed in and around a bench in the college gardens. She and Laurie were in the middle, both wearing their *Romeo and Juliet* T-shirts. Bobby, Laurie's boyfriend, was just at the side. There were half a dozen kids sitting on the grass in front, including Dodger, who was wearing a hat with a cloth axe sticking in the top.

To the right was Lesley, their tutor, standing stiffly, like a classroom teacher in a school photograph. Laurie and she had taken the mickey out of her because of that. Loosen up, they'd said, relax, this is just a snap for the album.

Jessie could remember it as though it was yesterday. Everyone had laughed. It had been sunny and there was a feeling of exhilaration in the air. It was three or four days until the end of term. There was the six-week holiday stretching out before them, no exams for another year.

After the photo had been taken, Laurie had pulled her to the side and said, "I feel so ... I don't know, I feel as if just anything could happen!"

"Are you still seeing Bobby?" Jessie had said, looking over at the fair-haired boy who was talking to his friend.

"Um ... maybe ... who knows?" she'd said mysteriously.

Dodger had come over then and put an arm round each of them.

"Coming for a beverage?" he'd said.

Laurie had laughed, shaken his arm off and turned away to talk to someone else but Jessie had gone with him. It was like Dodger to use odd words. Beverage; why couldn't he just say tea or coffee?

Jessie held tightly onto the photo.

Just three months later Laurie was dead.

Jessie sat in the chair beside her bed. She closed her eyes tightly even though she knew she had no tears left. It had been months since she had got upset about Laurie. A vague feeling of guilt seemed to surface somewhere in her chest.

As she put the photo back in the box a newspaper clipping caught her eye. She picked it up. There was a bold headline that said, "Romeo and Juliet Suicide". Underneath were the details. Jessie let the piece of paper drop from her hand. She knew the story, off by heart.

They had found Laurie in her car, an empty bottle of wine beside her on the seat, a note in an envelope for her boyfriend. She'd driven her car to a lonely cul-de-sac in Epping Forest and swallowed sleeping tablets, one after the other, washing them down with wine, straight out of the bottle.

Jessie had been in class when the news had come through. She'd been sitting behind Bobby Mathews listening to a lecture about the Industrial Revolution. She was making notes but every now and then she'd looked at the back of Bobby's neck, at the way his hair curled over his collar. In her book she wrote his name in the middle of her notes.

The Industrial Revolution Bobby brought great numbers of people Bobby together in one place Bobby.

The principal came into the room and took the teacher outside for a moment. While they were gone Bobby had turned round to Jessie and winked at her. She'd let the corners of her mouth move into a tiny smile but inside her chest there were fireworks igniting.

The teacher came back into the room and stopped the lesson. She'd started to speak but had had to stop after only a few words. Jessie had recognized Laurie's name.

Finally the teacher said, "There's been a terrible accident. Lauren Drake is dead."

There was a collective gasp. It was as though they were all watching someone walking on the high wire who had just lost their balance. Jessie had felt her mouth go dry and her eyes seemed to be locked onto the bit of paper in front of her. She'd looked at the strong black handwriting, "The Industrial Revolution." She'd watched the edges of the words fray and quiver and then the whole page began to blur.

The teacher had had to go out of the classroom and lots of the kids had sat in silent disbelief.

A year had passed since then.

The sound of a knock on her bedroom door made Jessie snatch up the newspaper clipping and shove it back into the box.

"Jessie, are you decent?" It was something her dad always said as he was about to come into her room.

"Yes."

"You all right love? Only you've been up here a long time."

"I'm fine. I was just looking at some stuff."

He sat down on the bed. "I know what today is," he said. "I haven't forgotten, you know."

Jessie grabbed his hand. She knew he'd remember. For months, especially after mum had left, she and Laurie had been real best friends. It had seemed as though she was part of the family, another daughter, a sister, not just a girl who lived a few streets away.

Her dad had been stunned when Laurie died.

"Why don't you come downstairs," he said. "There's some soup we can have for tea. Oh, by the way, this came for you. Must be from one of your young men."

Her dad stood up and handed her a letter. Jessie took it and lay it down on the bed.

"Soup, then?" her dad asked.

"I'll be down in a minute," she smiled. "I'm just finishing tidying up."

"Um . . ."

When she heard his footsteps on the stairs she sat down on the bed and looked at the envelope. The handwriting was the same, large loops on the "h" and the "p" and a long tail on the "y".

It was the fourth letter. The other three had come in the weeks following Laurie's death and she had thrown them away. The sight of his handwriting in those early weeks had made her feel nauseous and she hadn't wanted to read what he had to say.

He had lied to her, she was sure.

He had said that he and Laurie had been finished for months, that there was nothing between them.

But when the police had pulled Laurie out of her car, when they'd carried her stiff body to the pathologist for examination, they'd found out that she had been pregnant.

Laurie had got into her beaten-up car, driven to a spot in the middle of nowhere, taken a bottle of wine and some tablets. She'd fallen into a heavy sleep from which she'd never woken up and all the time there'd been a tiny baby growing inside her.

Bobby's baby, everyone had said. He had denied it.

Jessie had refused to see him, to hear his side of the story.

After the funeral he'd been off sick for weeks. He'd written to her but she'd thrown the letters away. One day she heard that he had left college, that he was working with his dad in the roofing business.

She'd seen him about a month before, in the precinct, with a fair-haired girl, who had her arm round his neck. She'd turned and looked in a shop window to avoid making contact with him.

And now the letter.

Jessie looked at the envelope. She pushed her thumb into the corner and ripped it apart.

Dear Jess, it said.

A year today and nothing was ever really sorted out. I saw Laurie's mum yesterday and she gave me a load of her stuff. There's some of my letters to her and a few small presents I bought her in the early days.

There's also some stuff in it that I don't think I was meant to see.

I know you'll think I'm silly but I never really believed that Laurie killed herself. The police thought differently though. Some of the things that Laurie's mum gave me have made me start thinking about it all again.

Not just that, but I've received something odd in the post.

Please see me, if only to talk me out of it once and for all. I'll be down at Murphy's early this evening.

Please come.

Bobby.

Jessie looked at her watch. It was five-thirty.
She had no intention of going to Murphy's.
It was the last thing she wanted to do.

2

Murphy's was unusually empty when Jessie walked in and looked around for Bobby. She couldn't see him among the boys playing cards or the knots of young men and women sitting in the booths by the window.

Her first impulse was to turn round and walk out again. She didn't though. She bought herself a coffee and sat in one of the soft seats. There was a newspaper lying on the table and she flicked over its pages.

She glanced through the pictures. In her head she was thinking about the first time she and Bobby had got together, there in Murphy's.

It had been the first weekend in September, a month or so before Laurie's suicide. They'd been sharing a pizza that had just come out of the oven and had been so hot that it burnt the inside of Bobby's lip. He had been talking about Laurie and what happened between them.

"Things were fine until she and the others went to Norfolk. I told her that the summer was too long for us to be apart. She just laughed. She said it would do us good, that we'd been seeing too much of each other anyway. I should've known then that she was fed up with me."

Jessie hadn't answered him. The truth was she didn't really know what Laurie had been thinking of for quite a while. She and Laurie had been drifting apart for months. They still chatted and rang each other from time to time but they weren't as close as they had once been. There hadn't been a point, a day, when they had stopped being "best friends". Laurie had Bobby and Jessie had started to pal around with a couple of girls in her English group.

The first time Jessie had heard of the break-up was when Laurie phoned her in the last week of the summer holidays, just after she'd returned from Norfolk.

"Do me a favour," she'd said. "See Bobby for me, will you? We're not seeing each other at the moment and he's making a bit of a nuisance of himself. Maybe if you talked to him . . ."

Jessie had been a bit annoyed. Apart from a

postcard it had been the first she had heard from Laurie for weeks.

In the end she and Bobby had gone to Murphy's. She'd listened and nodded when he'd talked about Laurie. He wasn't heartbroken, that was clear, but he was hurt and confused. Laurie had never exactly finished with him. She had just said that they should be alone for a bit.

After a while they'd started to talk about things other than Laurie. Bobby's passion for old Hollywood films, Jessie's plans to go to university.

About ten, they'd left. Bobby had walked her to the end of her road and said, "Thanks for the chat," and kissed her lightly on the cheek. His lips had brushed her skin and afterwards she'd kept touching the spot with her fingers and smiling to herself.

That had been the very first night.

Jessie stopped looking at the newspaper at the very moment that Bobby Mathews came into the café. He was flushed and his breathing was heavy, as though he'd been rushing. He looked around for a few seconds, his forehead pursed, as though he expected her not to be there.

When he saw her he smiled. In a few seconds he was standing by the table. In his hand was a plastic carrier bag.

"I'll just get a drink," he said and went off to the counter.

* * *

11

"I haven't come here to talk about us," Jessie said. She wanted to get things straight from the beginning.

"I know," he said.

"Whatever the rights and wrongs of it were it's all history now," she said. His hair was longer, she noticed, and it looked as though he was growing a moustache.

"I know," he said.

"I'm only here to talk about Laurie."

"So am I!" he said with a mocking smile on his face. "Look, I'm seeing someone now. I don't want to dredge up old times. It's Laurie I want to talk about."

"Good," she said, but a feeling of depression settled on her chest like a deflating balloon.

"That's settled then," he said and his blue eyes rested on her face.

They bought a plate of chips between them.

"Laurie's mum had a clear out of some of her things. She found the old brown suitcase that I'd bought Laurie from Camden Market when we'd started going out. You know, one of those old-fashioned ones. It cost me an arm and a leg." Bobby stopped and took a chip.

Jessie remembered the suitcase. They'd all been envious of it because it was so old. It was brown leather, hard to touch, and it had reinforced corners and two tiny fasteners with a key tied to the handle. It was too small actually to pack clothes in so Laurie had used it for her photos and letters.

"I thought the police searched through all of Laurie's things. How come they didn't look through the case?"

"They did look over her room and through her things, but not deeply, not thoroughly. Why should they? Laurie killed herself. There was no sign of a struggle or anyone else being involved. There was a suicide note written in her handwriting. Why should the police suspect foul play?"

He stopped speaking and leaned down to get the carrier bag that had collapsed onto the floor. "These are some of the things I found in the suitcase."

There were four small postcards, with prints of paintings on them. She recognized one of them because her dad had a large copy in his bedroom – it was a pond covered in water-lilies. She turned them over. On each card the word LAURIE had been printed with a message underneath. *LOVE YOU ALWAYS*; *YOU'VE CHANGED MY LIFE*; *YOU ARE MY SUNSHINE*; *COULDN'T SLEEP LAST NIGHT AFTER YOU HAD GONE*; *THOUGHT ABOUT YOU ALL DAY*.

The messages were printed in small neat capitals. There was no name or address on the right-hand side.

"These weren't posted, then?"

"No," Bobby said. "And they weren't from me."

He handed her another piece of paper. It was a partly-written letter and it was in Laurie's handwriting. On the top right-hand corner was a date, Oct 3rd, three days before she died.

"This was hidden in the lining of the suitcase. No one else has seen it," Bobby said.

> *My love*, it said.
>
> *You think you're making me unhappy but you're not. Knowing you has opened up my life. You're unhappy about the baby, I know. But for me it means everything. At first there'll be a lot of tears and anger, but once everyone knows they'll get used to the idea. I keep remembering the play last week, when Juliet said "Parting is such sweet sorrow." That's how I feel about you. I hear my mum coming up the stairs. I will finish this later . . .*

Jessie turned the page over but there was no more writing. She looked at Bobby. "What does it mean?" she said.

"It's not written to me, if that's what you think," he said.

"I've told you I'm not interested in what happened between you and Laurie last year. It's history."

"Let me explain, please," he said. Jessie sat back, the chips lying, going cold on the plate between them.

"Everyone, including you, thought that me and Laurie had been seeing each other last autumn. The truth is I did see her once. It was in the middle of September, when my parents went away for a weekend. It was just after you and I had had that long chat in here, the first time. She seemed really keen to see me and stayed over the night. She was bubbly and nice, like it was at the beginning, and I thought it was all on again. I saw her in college on the Monday but she couldn't see me because she was baby-sitting. Then she was away on the Tuesday and Wednesday and when I saw her on the Thursday she was cold and distant again, said she'd made a mistake." He stopped and began to fidget with the postcards, laying them out on the table in a straight line.

"Look . . ." Jessie said. She didn't want to hear. If he had made Laurie pregnant while he was seeing her, then she didn't want to know the details of it.

"No, let me finish. Please. The fact is that the police and the coroner thought that the suicide note was for her boyfriend, i.e. me. I tried to tell everyone at the time that she hadn't been upset over me. I also said that the baby couldn't have been mine. We'd only been together once between July and the time that she died!"

"It only takes once," Jessie said, pushing the plate of chips to the side.

"She had someone else, Jess. Someone that she was keeping quiet about, not me."

"But so what? That doesn't mean she didn't kill herself!"

"There's something else," Bobby said, getting an envelope out of his pocket. Jessie took it from him. It was addressed to him and she took the letter out.

She almost laughed when she first looked at it. It was like something out of a kidnap story in a film. It was a piece of white paper with words from a newspaper stuck on it.

She read it over a couple of times.

LAURIE DIDN'T KILL HERSELF. FIND THE MAN SHE WAS INVOLVED WITH. HE IS RESPONSIBLE FOR HER DEATH.

"I'm not the only one who thinks that something was going on."

"Maybe Laurie *was* involved with someone. Perhaps he *was* the father of her baby. There's probably nothing more to it than that. You've been watching too many old detective films."

"You've remembered the films I like then?" he said.

Of course she remembered them. Old black and white prints that they could only get in particular video shops. Films about men in trench coats and Trilby hats; women with hairstyles that stayed so firmly in place it looked as though they'd been sprayed on. The hero and heroine kissing in the last reel, when the mystery had been solved, their lips tightly closed and meeting briefly while the music rose to a feverish pitch.

"And what about this?" Bobby said, holding the note in mid-air, a look of stubbornness on his face.

"I don't know. Maybe it's someone playing a joke, being unkind. I'd take it to the police if I were you, let them look at it."

"No," he said. "If they take it over I'll never know what happened. They'll sweep it all under some carpet and close the file up again."

"Maybe that would be for the best," she said, looking straight at him.

3

Her radio alarm jolted her out of a deep sleep about seven o'clock. She sat bolt upright as though she were late for work. She rubbed her eyes with her fists. There were thoughts racing through her head and she felt as if she ought to get up that very minute.

Her bedroom door opened.

"You decent love?" Her dad came in with a mug of tea and put it down by the side of her bed. He had his running clothes on and she could see that his forehead was covered in sweat.

"Been running?" she said unnecessarily.

"Five miles, thirty-two minutes," he said, looking pleased with himself.

"There's a good boy," she said, rolling her eyes

and smiling. She picked up the mug of tea and took a scalding mouthful.

"I don't know how you can drink it that hot," her dad said. "You must be spitting out skin all day long."

She watched him go out the door and took another steaming mouthful.

Friday was a work day. She looked at her bedside clock. At seven-twenty she would jump out of bed and get ready. At seven-forty she would sit down and have some toast with her dad and a chat about the day ahead. She'd ask him what lessons he had to teach and he'd tell her about the terrible year nine class that he'd have or the awful girls' P.E. lesson that he'd have to cover. He'd ask her what she was going to do at lunch-time and she'd tell him, as she usually did, that she'd probably go to McDonalds with some of the girls from the supermarket and have a browse around the shops. At eight-fifteen they'd both be ready to leave. Her dad would give her a lift to the top of the High Street and then go on his way. At eight-thirty she'd clock on for her long day in the supermarket.

It was still only seven past seven though.

She lay back and thought about her talk with Bobby Mathews. All these problems over Laurie Drake. She'd have liked that, Laurie, being the centre of attention.

It was how they'd first got to know each other.

Laurie, in trouble, waiting outside the head teacher's door.

Jessie had a message for the head teacher from one of the teachers who was on break duty. It hadn't been something she'd volunteered for, she'd just been passing when Miss Henry had recognized her from the dozens of faces milling around.

"Jessica Morris, please take this to Mrs Peters. It's important that she gets it before the end of break."

And so Jessie had woven her way through the football and handball games, in between the weaving "hee" players and round the outside of the various quarrels and squabbles that were blossoming all over the playground. She'd gone straight up to the head's office and found an engaged sign on her door. *Do not enter*, it had said. A girl that she didn't know very well was sitting on one of the seats outside. She joined her on the next chair.

"Damn, damn, damn," the girl said. "This is the third time. I'm bound to get a letter home."

"What happened?" Jessie said.

"Got caught going to the shop."

"Oh."

Across the road from school was a small shop that sold everything from chocolate to wallpaper paste. Students weren't allowed to go out of school during break to get sweets or drinks although many did.

"I'd made sure the coast was clear and was just creeping out of the side door – you know, round by the dustbins – and old Henry appears out of nowhere. I nearly jumped out of my skin."

Jessie found herself laughing gently.

"She made me feel like I was a lifer escaping from some maximum security wing. You should have seen her, her face puffed up with glee, you know, that she'd caught me right in the act."

Jessie imagined Miss Henry standing at the side gates, a look of triumph on her face. It was only fair that she should have the odd victory. Most of the time she was on the losing side and any number of young girls or boys that she attempted to teach were the victors.

"I feel sorry for her sometimes," Jessie said, thinking of her standing, trying to guess the names of boisterous or cheeky pupils in order to try to control them. She had even seen her cry once.

"Feel sorry for her! What about me? When my dad gets this letter he's going to kill me and I'm not talking about a telling off."

They sat for a minute in silence. In the distance the shouts of the playing children sounded like the noise that comes from a swimming pool without the splashes.

Jessie unfolded the note in front of her. On it Miss Henry had scrawled, *Joanne Waters attempting to go off site*.

"You're not Joanne Waters!" she said, looking at the girl. Joanne was a very bright girl from year ten who was always carrying an instrument case of some sort around with her.

"Well spotted!" the girl said. "Laurie Drake, 10T."

Jessie introduced herself.

The bell rang above their heads and the noise of children from the playground moved closer into the building.

Jessie looked at the note. Taking a corner of it in each hand she began to tear it in half and then in half again.

They both tiptoed away from the head teacher's door.

"That's got me out of a lot of trouble," Laurie said on her way downstairs, "but what if old Henry follows it up?"

Jessie pointed towards the corridor leading to the staffroom. Miss Henry, her shoulders hunched as though she were expecting a weapon to hit her at any moment, was gathering speed until the staffroom door suddenly swallowed her up.

"No chance," Jessie said, "and if she does, I'm sure Joanne Waters will be able to explain her way out of it."

They both laughed out loud and walked off in different directions.

* * *

The supermarket was getting crowded and Jessie pushed her trolley of tins of tomatoes through the crowds until she reached the stand where she was supposed to stack them. All the way she kept being approached by shoppers asking, Where's the cheese? Have you any olives? Why have you moved the salami? Are you sure this is the right price? Where's the low-fat milk?

She'd tried to answer as best she could but after a while she wanted to scream out loud, *I don't know. Use your eyes. Can't you read?*

But she said none of these things. It was only a part-time job but she was lucky to have it. She would work at it until the following spring and try to get a summer job abroad, maybe in France. That would see her through until September when she would decide whether or not to take up her place for university.

It wasn't what she'd planned to do when she started at sixth-form college. None of them had. They'd all had firm ideas, her, Laurie, Dodger and Bobby.

A levels and then university. Good education, good jobs, the good things in life.

But when Laurie killed herself they had all seemed to lose their way. Bobby had dropped the course halfway, had given up all together. For months he had stopped going to the regular places that they'd all used. No one saw him around.

Some kids said that he'd started to reappear towards the summer, dropping in to Murphy's a couple of times. Dodger had stayed on a few months and then just stopped coming in. Lesley Bradley, their form tutor, had told them that he wasn't coming back. Jessie had seen him from time to time. He had a job in a record shop and then she'd seen him hanging out with a crowd of kids that she hadn't known.

Jessie had stayed on and finished her A levels. She'd been upset over Laurie's death but she hadn't missed her presence as she'd thought she would. For the first six months or so after the suicide she'd hung around with some new friends and for a while she'd gone out with a boy called Terry who was doing Business Studies. In the summer though, when the exams started to loom up, she'd begun to feel alone, panicky even. For about a week she'd gone to pieces, visited Laurie's grave a couple of times, gone to see her mum and dad, cried until her eyes were sore. Lesley Bradley had called it "delayed shock". She hadn't known what to call it, but it had stopped her thinkng about the future – university or careers.

Jessie stacked the tomato tins into a pyramid at the corner of an aisle. She was asking for trouble doing it this way; someone was bound to knock it down with their trolley or some young child would career into it. She shrugged her shoulders.

She wondered whether Bobby was perched on a roof at that very minute, handing his dad roof tiles, balancing so that he didn't fall down.

"My dad wants me to go into business with him," he'd said to her, on the first real date they'd had, not in Murphy's but in an Indian restaurant. "I don't want to spend my life doing that!" He'd said it incredulously, as though it was out of the question.

A great feeling of emptiness swirled in her stomach. In her hands she held two tins of tomatoes, ideal for soups, casseroles, sauces, it said on the label. Bobby Mathews had somebody new, he had told her.

She could still ring him though, they were old friends.

She could still get in touch with him, just to see if he had found out anything more about Laurie's death.

That evening, while her dad was marking books in his room, she got out her address book and dialled his number.

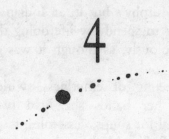

4

"Jessie, this is Anne. Anne this is Jessie, who I told you about, Laurie's friend."

Jessie nodded at the fair-haired girl on the other side of the table. A waitress came up and she asked for a cup of lemon tea.

"I bumped into Anne on my way here. She fancied a coffee so I brought her along. She wanted to meet you anyway." Bobby was talking quickly, gesticulating with his hands. Jessie could see them trembling slightly. He was clearly nervous. He turned to Anne whose face was partly hidden by a mug of coffee. "Jessie was Laurie's best friend. That's why I contacted her when I found the stuff in the suitcase and got that letter. If anyone is interested in finding out the truth she is."

Anne said nothing but her large eyes swivelled round to settle on Jessie. Bobby hadn't told her about their past relationship, that was clear. Bobby was introducing her as a friend of Laurie's, that was all.

Bobby looked beseechingly at Jessie. He wanted her to speak, to give weight to his story. She said nothing.

"What do you think about all this?" Anne eventually said, opening her bag and pulling out a black purse.

"I'm not sure," Jessie said. "I think it may add up to nothing. On the other hand . . ."

Anne pulled out some pound coins and put them on a saucer. Jessie heard them clatter one by one. Anne's hand was shaking very slightly as well. She was clearly nervous. Her boyfriend had dredged someone up from his past and she wasn't clear what it was all about.

Jessie felt sorry for her. "I can't stay very long though, Bobby. I'm meeting my boyfriend in an hour or so."

Boyfriend?

"Boyfriend?" they both said. Anne's face relaxed, Bobby's forehead wrinkled.

"Yes, we're going shopping," she said.

"What's his name?" Anne said, a wide smile on her face.

Jessie looked around the coffee shop. A sign on

the wall said, *Try Toni's Italian Ice Creams*.

"Tony," she said, as Anne was getting up from her seat.

"That's nice. Well I'd better go, I'm on a late lunch. See you tonight," she said to Bobby, kissing him gently on the head.

"Yes, about nine."

"You never said you were seeing someone new," Bobby said when she had gone. His fingers were tapping a rhythm on the table.

"You never asked," Jessie said, as the waitress brought her tea.

Later, walking through the shopping centre, they came to a bench beside an ornamental pool. At the bottom of the pool were thousands of copper-coloured coins. One young boy was rolling his sleeve up and surreptitiously dipping his arm in.

"If Laurie was keeping her love affair secret it must mean that the man in question was out of bounds. He may have been married."

"Not necessarily," Jessie said. "She could have just been keeping it from you. Maybe she didn't want you to get upset."

"But she didn't tell anyone. Anyway, she knew that you and I were seeing each other. She finished with me! Why should she worry about my feelings?"

Jessie was quiet for a moment. Laurie had been

one of her best friends. Why hadn't she told her about the new man in her life?

"She would have told me," Jessie said, her voice trailing off at the end. Would she have told her? It had been a long time since they had been really close.

"And then there's the anonymous note," Bobby said, as if he was laying a final playing-card down on an imaginary table.

"The question is, how are we going to find out?" Jessie said, her voice weary.

"Dodger might know," Bobby said. "During those last few weeks she was always sitting with Dodger in college or hanging around with him in Murphy's, don't you remember?"

"Yes," Jessie said. She and Bobby used to see them when they went in there together. It all seemed like a million years ago.

Jessie looked straight ahead at the young boy pulling his wet arm out of the pool, his face red from the exertion of trying to reach a coin. She could feel Bobby looking at her, his eyes willing her to turn round and answer him, look at him.

"They're for charity," she shouted and the young boy turned round and gave her a scowl. He continued to dip his arm in the water.

"You'll have to talk to Dodger," Bobby said finally. "Me and him never got on all that well, especially not towards the end."

Jessie got up and walked across to the young boy. She bent and whispered in his ear, "If you don't stop trying to nick this money *now*, my friend and I will see to it that your whole body is immersed in water."

The boy drew a large sigh, rolled his sleeve down and swore.

Jessie stood for a moment, watching him walk away, his shoulders and back straight, as though he had a broomstick up his coat.

For a moment he reminded her of Dodger and his cocky walk, oozing with self-confidence.

"I'll talk to Dodger," she said without looking round. "What will you do?"

"A mate of mine is a cadet, down at the central police station. He says he'll see what he can find out."

"OK," she said. "I'll be in touch." And she walked away.

5

The record shop was in a side street off the High Road. It dealt in specialist soul music, the kind of stuff that Dodger liked a lot.

Jessie walked around for a while, looking at the stalls in the market deciding what to say to Dodger.

We think Laurie's death was suspicious and we'd like you to help us with our enquiries.

When did you last see Laurie Drake?

Have you an alibi for the weekend of her supposed suicide?

Was there anything between you and Laurie Drake?

We have received an anonymous note that suggests . . .

She found herself smiling at these pathetic phrases. They made her sound like an amateur Miss Marple.

A vague feeling of guilt niggled at her stomach and she turned into the street that the record shop was in. None of it was very funny. Laurie Drake, her one-time best friend had died in odd circumstances. Everyone thought it was suicide. Bobby Mathews did not. She was helping him find out what he could about the death.

But was she?

Was she really interested in Laurie's death?

She thought of Bobby Mathews' girlfriend, Anne. She'd kissed him lightly on the head, an act that said, I own this man, keep away from him.

Had Laurie ever kissed him like that? Had she, herself, ever kissed him like that when they had been together for those few short weeks?

Jessie pushed open the door of the record store. She was hit by the throbbing sounds of reggae music. She looked around the store for Dodger's face but couldn't see him.

"Is Dodger around?" she said to a pale young man behind the counter.

"Dodger?" he said.

"I mean Trevor," she said. "Does he still work here? I haven't seen him for a while . . ."

"Trev? Nah, he hasn't worked here for . . . let me see . . . three months or more . . . that right Shirl?" he called to a woman who was squatting down beside a pile of CDs on the floor.

"Trev?" she said, without looking round. "Trev

got some labouring on the new precinct. About June or July I think."

"Thanks," Jessie said, dismayed. "You haven't got a phone number?"

"Phone number? You hear that Shirl. Young lady wants to know if Trev has a *phone* number!"

The young woman laughed. Jessie began to feel annoyed. "Look, I just want to get in touch with him. It's important."

"Try the squat down at the old council estate. Last I heard he was living there."

"Thanks," Jessie said and walked out.

Jessie signed her name on the till roll and sat behind the checkout. Sarah, a girl that she occasionally went out with, was on the till next to hers.

"Coming to the pictures Friday, Jess?" she said holding a packet of pasta in mid-air for a price.

"Possibly," Jessie said. Pictures and an Indian meal on Friday nights. A few drinks on Saturday, maybe a party in someone's house. It had been her social life for the last few months and she was fed up with it. Hanging around with girls and boys whose main conversations were centred around what they were wearing and what car they'd like to buy, if they could afford it.

Had she and Laurie and the others been any different though? Hadn't they talked about those things? She remembered Dodger going on about convertible BMWs and Laurie ringing her up excitedly to tell her she'd just bought some new jeans or shoes.

A woman approached with a trolley that was loaded to the top. In the child seat was a small toddler arching its back in an attempt to escape. The woman was throwing her shopping onto the moving belt and saying, "Be a good girl, poppet, just for Mummy."

Jessie sighed and began to pick up the first items of shopping. She passed them lazily over the scanner and heard a small "bip" every time a bar-code was read. Her arms reached out robotically and placed the shopping onto the moving rail behind her where it piled up clumsily in a corner.

"Please be a good girl, poppet, just for Mummy," she could hear the woman's words receding into the distance and she began to think about Dodger.

She and Laurie had been in the college canteen on the first day of the term when a short, stocky lad had sat opposite them and introduced himself.

"Trevor Billings," he'd said. "Most people call me Dodger. I'm a stereotype, from a single parent family, my mother, bless her heart. Interests? Body building, soul music and getting on in life."

They'd looked aghast and he'd taken a bite from a roll and said, "'OK, etiquette being what it is, it's your turn to tell me about yourselves."

They'd laughed, but they'd introduced themselves. That was what Dodger had been like, brash and confident.

Jessie felt herself smiling at the memory. A voice broke into her thoughts.

"Here's my cheque, dear." The woman was holding the cheque and card out and using her other hand to stroke the toddler's head.

Jessie checked the date and signature. Then she wrote the card number on the back.

The toddler had her fist in her mouth and was moaning deeply.

"All right, poppet," the woman said, replacing her card in her purse and pushing the trolley off.

Jessie looked at her watch. She had forty minutes to go and then her dad would pick her up.

It was one of the things that she and Dodger now had in common. She was now the "child" of a broken family. Of course it had been years since Dodger's dad left home; her own mum had only been gone just under two years. She thought of her dad at home at that minute, putting something into the oven for her tea, a pie or a chilled meal. Then he'd wipe over the kitchen surfaces and dry up any dishes that he'd dirtied.

He might do some reading or listen to the radio or one of his CDs.

She felt a surge of sadness at this picture of him, leading a solitary life, with only his daughter to look after.

What would happen when she was gone? When he was really alone?

Dodger had left home, she had heard, soon after he left college. His mum had a boyfriend though, that had been one of the problems. Would her dad ever have a girlfriend?

In the back of her head she heard, "Do you take vouchers, dear? I say, dear, do you take these vouchers?" She saw a small, thin, grey-haired woman in front of her, her basket appearing to be full of cat food and mineral water.

"Yes, we do," she said, reaching for the tins. In her head she held a picture of her dad with a shadowy woman by his side.

6

Dodger was harder to find than she'd thought. He'd only stayed at the precinct building project for about six weeks. The council squat had been deserted. Someone said that the police had cleared it out a couple of weeks before and people had had to find other places to stay.

Jessie wondered whether Dodger would have gone back to his mum's. She thought not though, she had heard that there'd been rows. It was unlikely that Dodger would have been welcome, particularly if it was true that his mum had got a new boyfriend who was only a year or two older than Dodger himself.

In the end she'd remembered Sammy's Pool Rooms in the arches under the railway line.

She walked into the dark interior and looked from corner to corner, her eyes scanning the eight pool tables, each in a different stage of play.

She saw him leaning against the wall, over by the jukebox. As she walked round the tables, one or two of the young men looked up and made some comments that she ignored. Dodger was intent on a game that was going on on the table in front of him. She walked up to within a metre or so of him before he noticed anything.

He looked up and stood back to let her pass.

"Dodger, it's me," she said. He seemed to drag his eyes off the table and turn them slowly to look at her face.

"Jess," he said and looked puzzled.

"Dodger," she smiled. He looked drunk. "Could we go for a cup of coffee somewhere? I've got some things to ask you."

They walked out into the daylight. Jessie went first and turned round to wait for Dodger to catch her up.

In the daylight he looked awful. His clothes were wrinkled and grubby. His hair was longer and greasy. He was blinking and rubbing his eyes as though he hadn't been out for days. He looked heavier as well, as though he had a beer gut.

He shuffled up to her. "Where do you want to go," he said, the beginnings of a yawn making him stretch his arms up to the sky.

"Let's go to Jack's," she said and led the way.

Jack's was a café in an old part of the market. Since the new shopping precinct had been built the whole area had declined, many of the shops going out of business. The café stayed open though and was used mainly by bus drivers and workmen who were finishing off sections of the new precinct.

Jessie sat at a table and Dodger went up to the counter to buy the teas.

Jessie felt low. It was months and months since she'd seen Dodger and yet they'd had virtually nothing to say to each other. That, plus the fact that Dodger looked so awful, overweight and unkempt.

They'd been close once though. Right at the beginning of that first term, before Laurie had started to go out with Bobby. They'd met for coffee in the refectory and spent free lessons together in the common room.

Dodger had made them all laugh with his impressions of the tutors and of other students, particularly those who fancied themselves. The glamorous girls who spent hours putting make-up on or the tall, well-built boys who posed out on the college front lawn so that everyone could see them.

Laurie and she had laughed heartily, neither of them being potential oil paintings themselves. And Dodger, small and dark with shoulders like girders.

For a while, Jessie had thought that Dodger would ask Laurie to go out with him. Once he'd asked her advice about it.

"Look Jess, do you think she'd be interested, if I asked her out like. . . ?"

Jessie couldn't exactly remember what she'd said, give it a try or go ahead or something like that. It was at a Christmas party that he'd decided to pluck up courage and do it.

Jessie had been in the kitchen when Laurie had come running in, a half moon smile on her face.

"Guess what, guess what?" she'd said. "Guess who's asked me out?" Laurie was almost jumping on the spot. Jessie had been about to answer when Bobby Mathews had walked into the kitchen with Laurie's coat over his arm.

After they left, Dodger walked Jessie the few streets to her house. He gave her a peck on the cheek. "You win some, you lose some," he'd said and she'd watched him straighten his shoulders and walk back along her street towards the High Road.

He carried the teas back to their table and sat opposite her.

"So how's tricks?" he said and sipped his tea. She noticed the cup shaking in his hand.

"Where are you living?" she said.

"Here and there." He smiled and shrugged his shoulders.

"You mean nowhere?"

"I'm all right. I'm managing."

"Your mum?"

"Got married a month ago."

"Oh."

Jessie drank her tea. Where should she start? Before she could say anything Dodger spoke.

"A year ago last week. She's been dead a whole year."

"Yes," Jessie said. "I wanted to talk to you about her."

"Really?" Dodger said, putting his cup down on the table surface instead of in the saucer. He looked straight at her.

"About those last few months. I know you spent a lot of time with her. I just wondered . . ." She stopped in order to give him time to say something. He was silent though, just looking at her. "You and she were friends, I know, and she wasn't really close to anyone else . . ." She stopped again, hoping that he would start to talk, take up the threads of what she was saying. He didn't though. He started to sniff and she watched with dismay as he used his sleeve to wipe his nose. "It's just that we, I mean me and Bobby, we are beginning to wonder if there wasn't more to her death than—"

"Than?" he said quickly and raised his eyebrows. "Than meets the eye?" He was smiling. He was making fun of her. She felt suddenly angry. She'd spent a lot of time trying to find him.

"Don't bother!" she said and began to put her jacket on.

"No." He raised his voice suddenly. "No, you don't bother! Don't you bother asking me about her. She wasn't worth the worry, she wasn't. She was worth nothing. Sweet nothing."

He stood up suddenly, edging the table closer to her. His face was grey and for the first time Jessie noticed that his trousers were done up with a safety pin at the top. He began to walk away from the table but then he turned round.

"Do you know something?" he said. "When she died I was glad, I was. I celebrated when she died."

He walked away and let the door of the café slam behind him so that the woman behind the counter said, "That door, my God!"

Jessie sat for a few seconds before she realized that she was holding her breath. She let it go in one long exhalation and looked out into the street. There was no sign of him.

7

Her dad was in when she got home. She hung her coat in the hall cupboard and wondered what to do about Dodger.

A mood of depression seemed to be settling on her. Dodger had looked so awful! And the things he had said about Laurie. She had always known that he'd been upset because Laurie wouldn't go out with him, but she'd thought he'd got over it. Dodger was like that. He always had a joke up his sleeve, he didn't get upset if the other kids ribbed him about his height or the hats he wore.

But Dodger had changed. Had he meant what he said about Laurie? Had he hated her?

Her dad was reading something at the kitchen table.

"Cup of tea?" she said, lifting up the kettle.

"No. Thanks anyway," he said and began shuffling the papers in front of him. He looked fed up. She noticed he had a new shirt on, darkly coloured, and his tie was one she hadn't seen before.

Plugging the kettle in she recalled him buying a jacket the previous week that she wouldn't have minded wearing herself. He was quite good-looking really for someone of his age. Something Laurie once said came into her mind.

"Your dad doesn't look or act like someone's dad, not like mine, bald and fat and always preaching."

That had been when Laurie had first met him, before her mum had left. Jessie poured the boiling water onto the tea-bag and then mixed it round with a spoon. She lifted the soggy mass and dropped it into the bin. She was just about to sit down and talk to her dad when he stood up.

"I've got a couple of things to do on the computer. Then we'll start tea OK?" he said. He was using his fists to rub his eyes. He looked tired, even though it was only early evening.

He left some of his papers on the table and she looked at the top sheet. *National Curriculum Guidelines*, it said and she pushed them away and sipped her tea. A corner of blue caught her eye and she put her fingers underneath the pile of documents and picked out a blue envelope.

It was addressed to her father and it was her

mother's handwriting. That was why he looked unhappy. She shouldn't read it. She put it down again.

Still, after almost two years, her mother's presence – even in the form of a letter – could cause unhappiness. How long would it take before her dad got over it?

It was just after the first Christmas at college that her mum left home.

"She'll be back, Dad," Jessie said. "She's just confused. She just needs time alone, to sort herself out," Jessie said, repeating the phrases that her mum had said to her the weekend before.

Her mum had sat in the big armchair in the living-room and told her she was leaving that evening. Jessie remembered it well because she'd been sitting in the special chair that they all took turns to sit on, the one they all argued over, the most comfortable one. Her mum had sat in that chair, crossed her legs, played with the ends of a silk scarf that she had been wearing and told her that she didn't want to live with her dad any more.

Jessie had sat on the arm of the chair and leant her arm on her mother's shoulder.

"Have you had a row?" she had said, looking deep into the swirling patterns on the silk scarf that was hanging down from her mother's neck.

"No, no. If only it was as simple as that."

Her dad had been out all day with his running club.

"Is it because he's gone running?" she said, touching the end of the scarf with her finger and thumb. It was a stupid thing to say and she'd known it as soon as the words came out of her mouth. Grown up people didn't split up over things like that. It was the kind of thing a six year old would have said. Her mother shook her head and didn't answer. She didn't need to. Jessie sat, balancing on the arm of the special chair and wondered what her dad was doing at that very moment. Her mother's perfume was strong and from the side she could see some smudged mascara just under her lower eyelashes.

She opened her mouth to say a couple of things like, you can't, or what about me, or Dad and me need you, but nothing came out and she sat like a goldfish, holding onto her mother by the ends of a paisley-patterned scarf that felt cold and slippery on her fingers.

Every day for the following week her mother came back to see if they were all right. Once or twice she brought some groceries or collected a couple of things from her cupboards.

She'd sit for a while at the kitchen table and talk. Her dad would get up and make the tea.

"What's the flat like?" he'd say.

"Get to work all right from there?" he'd say.

"Need any help to take your things?" he'd say and hand her a mug of tea.

Jessie usually stayed for about ten minutes and then left them on their own. She'd go upstairs and listen from the landing or get her coat and walk round to Laurie's.

"I can't believe it!" Laurie had said. "Your mum and dad seemed to get on so well. Now my dad, I could imagine anyone leaving him, miserable old sod. But your dad!"

A month or so after she left the truth came out.

She came home from college and no one was in. That was unusual, her dad normally said if he was going to be late. She got herself some tea and put the telly on. She rang her mum's new flat to see if he was there but there was no answer.

At ten 'o clock she was getting worried. She rang Laurie and about ten minutes later she came round.

"He's probably gone for a drink with his friends from work. Maybe he's just forgotten to phone. He'll be in soon."

He came in just after eleven. He was drunk. His face was crimson and his eyes swivelled back and forth. He walked into the living-room and lay back in the big armchair.

"She's got someone else. All that stuff, about finding herself, being alone for a while, it was all cobblers!"

Laurie sat down on the arm of the chair, beside

him. Jessie stood in the middle of the room, her hands loosely clasped as though she were about to recite something.

She'd never seen her dad so obviously out of control. His tie had disappeared, his jacket looked stained and he was waving his arm about.

"I saw her! In a car with her boyfriend. A nice quiet alleyway. They thought no one could see them, but I could!"

He had seen her mum with another man. Jessie stiffened her back and took a deep breath. Laurie was patting her dad's hand, the one he had been waving about. She was saying "shh" as though her dad was a small kid who had just fallen over.

"I don't understand," Jessie said. "Where?"

"I followed her. See? I waited until she came out of work and got into her car and I followed her like a private detective."

Jessie's knees began to bend involuntarily. She leaned across to the mantelpiece.

"You followed her? A boyfriend?" she said and Laurie got up and came across to her.

"I'll make some tea," Laurie said, an embarrassed expression forming on her face.

It was then that they both heard the low wail of her dad's voice as he began to cry. His mouth was covered by one of his hands. The other hand was screwed up into a fist and he used it to beat the arm of the chair.

The special chair, the one they all used to fight over.

Jessie picked up the blue envelope with her mother's handwriting on. She wondered what was in the letter. It would only take a moment to open it. After all, she knew just about everything there was to know about the break-up. She'd heard it all over and over again in the weeks after the truth had come out.

At first her dad wouldn't even go to work.

"What's the point?" he said.

Laurie came round a lot. They'd decided between them that it was the best thing. When Laurie was there her dad stopped moping, if only because he was too polite or too proud to do it in front of her friend.

Laurie used to talk about her own dad, the councillor.

"He's such a hypocrite! Always at church talking about charity and helping your neighbour and the next minute he's in a meeting cutting back meals-on-wheels or day centres or something like that!"

Or her mum.

"House proud! She hoovers three times a day. She actually owns two vacuum cleaners, an upstairs one and a downstairs one. If I stood still for too long I'd probably be sucked up into one or other of them!"

Sometimes her dad laughed. Once or twice he looked quite cheerful and joined in the conversation, telling a couple of jokes. After a couple of weeks he did go back to work.

From time to time though, Jessie would happen on him, his eyes glittering and his face red where he had been crying. She heard the sounds of old songs coming from his room and found photos of her mum under his pillow when she was changing his sheets.

Two or three times a week Laurie Drake would come round and sit for a couple of hours watching the TV and chatting. Her dad seemed to cheer up and sometimes they would play cards or Trivial Pursuit.

Some friends from his running club came round and persuaded him to start training again for the Norwich half marathon that was going to be held in August. He began to go out more and occasionally he went for a drink with some friends from work.

He even went on a date once. A woman from work asked him to go and see a play with her but he never said anything about it and he never went out with her again.

Laurie came round once or twice and he wasn't in.

"You know," she said, one evening when she and Jessie were watching a film. "You know, I miss not seeing your dad so much now that he's got over it all. He was really good company!"

Jessie nodded, but in her head she wondered if he would ever really get over it.

"What shall we eat then?" her dad said.

"I don't mind," Jessie said, pushing the blue envelope back under the documents on the table.

"We could have . . . frozen pie and chips . . . or chips and frozen pie?"

"Um . . ." Jessie screwed her mouth up. "Let me see . . . I think we should have frozen pie and chips, don't you?"

8

Bobby Mathews' expression darkened when she told him about Dodger.

"Celebrate?" he said. "I don't get it. I knew he liked her once, but she was never interested in him. That's why I wasn't worried when she wrote and told me he was in Norfolk with her."

"Dodger went to Norfolk?"

"Yeah, he got a job at the last minute. Someone else pulled out. I thought you probably knew."

Jessie hadn't known. Once Laurie had got the job in the Outdoor Pursuits camp in Cromer she had hardly seen her.

They stood in silence for a few moments. Bobby was staring across the street where his dad and another man were unloading roof tiles into a front garden.

"Did you get anything from your mate in the police?" she said, uneasy at the silence.

He looked back at her and she could see that he was momentarily distracted. He was thinking of something else. For a moment he looked as though he hadn't heard her then he said, "What?"

"Your mate, the police cadet."

"Yes," he said. "Not much but a couple of things."

"Bobbo?" his dad called across the road.

"Look, I've got an idea, a theory really," he said. "Could you come round to my place tonight. I'll try it out on you. About eight?"

Before she had a chance to answer he was gone.

She turned and walked off towards the shopping centre.

Inside the shopping centre it was warm and bright. There were giant palm trees that reached up to the next floor and hanging green plants from each balcony.

She found herself looking into shop windows even though she had no money to buy. She caught her own reflection in the window, her hair looking as though it needed a cut, her clothes limp, her shoulders round.

Was Bobby Mathews still seeing his girlfriend, Anne?

Would he tell her that he had invited Jessie round for the evening?

She walked on and smiled to herself. She was getting carried away. She hadn't been invited for the evening. He'd just asked her to come round to hear some information he had. That was all. Maybe Anne would even be there!

Did she care?

These questions were buzzing around her head until she heard her name being called from a distance.

"Jessica. Jessica Morris."

She looked round but couldn't see anyone she knew. A woman with a pushchair came towards her. There was a man walking with her holding a toddler in his arms.

"Jessica. It's me, Lesley Bradley."

"Lesley," Jessie said it slowly, convinced that she didn't know anyone of that name. Then she remembered her old tutor. "Oh, Lesley, I'm so sorry I didn't recognize you, like this I mean . . ."

"It's all right. I'm out of context. You were used to seeing me as your teacher, not the mum of some small brats!" She laughed and the man with the toddler stood still.

"Oh, you've met Tom, my husband?" Jessie nodded and Lesley turned to the man. "Do you remember Jessica? She was one of my students. She was also one of Laurie Drake's best friends."

The man nodded, but the toddler had its hands on his face. He looked at Lesley. "A terrible business," he said.

"Tom knew Laurie because she baby-sat for this horror a few times." Lesley Bradley held her arms out and the toddler leaned across and grabbed onto her mother. The man took the pushchair while the toddler hugged and kissed her mother.

Jessie looked at the baby, sleeping in the buggy. It was about six months old.

"Have you gone back to college yet?" Jessie said.

"No, after Christmas. I thought I'd have the whole year off this time. Mind you, it's not exactly like 'time off'. It's the hardest work I've ever done, looking after two small kids. Tom helps, when he's at home." Jessie nodded. "I do get fed up though. Why don't you come round and see me? I still live in Rosemary Avenue, just down by the park. You remember?"

"Yes." Jessie had been to Lesley's house a couple of times during that first year at college.

"Come next week," Lesley said. Her husband, Tom, was starting to wheel the pushchair off in the direction of Woolworth's.

"OK," Jessie said. "When?"

"Tuesday. Come for lunch."

"See you then." Jessie watched Lesley Bradley catch up with her husband and the buggy. Then she walked off in the other direction.

9

Bobby was alone when she called at his house. He took her into the kitchen.

"Would you like some tea, coffee?"

"A coffee would be nice," she said, looking around the room, awkward at being in his house for the first time in over a year.

"Where're your mum and dad?"

"Me mum's gone to an evening class and Dad's down at the Three Feathers."

"Evening class?" Jessie imagined Bobby's mum doing cookery or flower arranging.

"Yeah. European History, can you believe it! She's always making me read her essays."

"You were quite good at that, as I recall," she said.

"A lot of good it did me." He was spooning some coffee into a cafetière. "If I'd gone straight into business with my dad, instead of going to that college, I'd have my own flat and car now. I'd be booking up holidays and buying designer clothes!"

He smiled and poured some boiling water into the glass cafetière. He lifted some mugs off the draining board and said, "Milk and sugar?"

"Just milk," she said, a mild disappointment niggling her that he hadn't remembered.

"I wouldn't be worrying about all this either," he said, pressing on the plunger. Jessie looked at the brown liquid bubbling up inside the cafetière. He poured the coffee and brought it over. He sat opposite her and she looked straight at him over the top of her mug. His hair was shorter now and his skin was still lightly tanned from the summer. She wanted to reach over and touch his face but felt a blush gurgling in her cheeks at the thought of it.

"How's Anne?" she said, wanting him to say, Oh that's all over, or it's nothing.

"She's fine," he said instead. She swallowed a large mouthful of the steaming coffee. He meant it then, when he'd said it was only Laurie's death he was interested in, not her, not them.

She put her mug down, looked at her watch and in a businesslike voice said, "What's your theory, then?"

"Right. First things first." Bobby picked up an envelope file that had been on the table. He took some papers out of it. "My dad's mate's son, Tony, is a cadet, so he don't get to see much. Most of the information about particular cases is on the computer any road, and you'd need a code word to access it. But what he did do was to talk to one of the CID officers who had been on the case. He told him that he'd known Laurie, et cetera. Anyway, this man told him a couple of things that he remembered."

"Are they allowed to talk about that stuff?"

"Not really, but it was only to another copper. He didn't know that Tony was going to tell me."

"Oh."

"The suicide note I'd already heard, read out at the coroner's inquest. Here, I've written the words down anyway." He handed Jessie a piece of paper. On it were the words of Laurie's suicide note, written by Bobby. It made her feel funny to read it.

Remember what Juliet says. Farewell! God knows when we shall meet again. I love you.
Laurie XXX

Jessie read it over a couple of times. It wasn't the first time she had heard it. Laurie's mum had told her what it had said straight after the suicide. As well as that, it had been all over the local papers: "Romeo and Juliet Suicide."

"Did she ever do that to you?" Jessie said. "I mean, quote lines from Shakespeare plays."

"Just *Romeo and Juliet*," he said, "in the early days. You remember she had a thing about the play."

"Yes."

Jessie did remember. They'd studied it in English and had seen a production of it in London as well as an old film of it. Laurie had written reams of notes on it and an extra essay, she'd liked it so much.

"Read the book, seen the film, heard the record, got the car sticker?" Dodger had said once, when she'd been going on about it. Laurie had just laughed and ignored the remark.

"The note was in an envelope. There was no writing on the outside," Bobby said. He laid another piece of notepaper in front of her. The words "position of body" were written at the top of a list. Jessie felt a lead weight descend down on her chest. A body. Laurie Drake was just a body.

"What's this?" she said, finishing the coffee.

"This is a list of things that the police found in the car."

Jessie's eyes scanned the page. An empty wine bottle, a corkscrew, a walkman with two cassette tapes, a shoulder bag in which there was a purse and some make-up, a child's toy.

"She had the troll with her?" she asked. Jessie

remembered it, an ugly toy with a shock of luminous pink hair sprouting from its plastic head. It was dressed in shorts and a T-shirt and had a tiny rucksack on its back. Laurie said it was her good luck mascot; she'd used it when taking her GCSEs and when she took her driving test.

"Exactly," Bobby said, his finger pointing into the air. "Why take a good luck charm with you if you're going to commit suicide, see? It doesn't make sense."

"Is that your theory?" Jessie said, more sharply than she'd meant to.

"And other things," he said. He began to arrange his bits of paper into an order.

"Look," Jessie fidgeted with the handle of her coffee mug. "Laurie was pregnant. Her dad was, is, a councillor, a church man. Her mum the house-proud type, worried about the neighbours."

"Come on. Thirty years ago I'd have agreed with you, even twenty years ago. But these days? She could have got an abortion. No one would have known. Young girls don't commit suicide because they're pregnant. Look . . ." Bobby stopped for a moment and took a couple of deep breaths. "Look, there's a couple of other small things that add up. The suicide note, the goodbye note. It doesn't actually mention her killing herself. It could have been a note she'd written any time."

"But . . ."

"And there was no container for the sleeping tablets, yet apparently she must have taken about a dozen. How did she carry them there?" Bobby's voice was getting higher and more excited.

"In her bag, in her pocket . . ." Jessie was speaking rapidly, feeling uncomfortable at Bobby's growing frustration.

"And," he said, not listening to her, "they found her in the passenger seat, not the driver's seat. Why did she change seats?" Bobby stood up and walked across to the window. Jessie followed him.

"At the time, I remember feeling uneasy about a couple of things but the police said that there was no sign of a struggle. Only her fingerprints were on the wine bottle. The note sounded a bit odd but that was put down to the fact that it was an unstable teenage girl that they were dealing with." Bobby's arm was shaking. "You know what I think?" he said, and leant back against the window. "I think there was someone there with her. Someone, the man she was involved with, was fed up with her, wanted her to leave him alone. I think he knew she wasn't going to give him up that easy. He put the sleeping tablets into the wine and then when she was asleep he wiped his prints off the bottle and placed her fingers back on it."

"Bobby, this is a bit far-fetched."

"He took the container of the tablets away in his pocket and put the note on to the dashboard and left her there to die. He knew that the police would accept the whole thing at face value."

He stopped and put his head against the window pane. Jessie lifted her arm and touched his shoulder.

"And we're not the only ones; someone else knows." He pulled the anonymous note out of his pocket. Jessie could see the stuck-on bits of newspaper.

He was being a detective, like one of those in the old films he liked.

She took the bit of paper from him. The only words she could see clearly were, *LAURIE DIDN'T KILL HERSELF.* She let the paper drop on to the kitchen unit behind her.

He sighed and raised his eyebrows at her.

"You think I'm silly," he said.

Her face was just centimetres from his. She raised her arm and began to stroke his hair. She could feel him relax and without thinking she closed her eyes and leant forward to kiss him. She felt his lips part slightly and his head lean back as she used her free hand to touch his neck.

One moment there was a buzz in her chest as she felt the warmth of his mouth and then suddenly his hands were on her shoulders and he was holding her away from him.

"I'm sorry, Jess. This is not what I meant. I thought you understood."

She felt her face heating up and she knew that her mouth was hanging open.

She turned round.

"I must go," she said, looking for her jacket.

"I'm sorry," he said. On the table were the bits of paper that he had written his notes on and two empty coffee mugs. She picked up her bag from the floor.

"I'm sorry." She heard his words as she pulled the front door shut behind her and walked quickly along the street.

10

Idiot! Fool! She repeated these words over to herself as she half walked, half ran the distance between Bobby's house and her own.

Pathetic. Stupid. She stopped for a few seconds when she was well away from his street and leaned back against a wall.

Bobby had never got over Laurie.

Even last year, when they were going out together, he was pining for her, grieving for her and she wasn't even dead.

She walked the rest of the way home, letting the crisp autumn air cool her face.

Five weeks they'd been together, although to her, it had seemed like months. Three or four meetings in Murphy's, a couple of Indian meals, hours traipsing round video shops looking for detective films, evenings spent in his house, listening to music, holding each other close.

He had never said anything about his feelings for her though. He'd kissed her, held her hand, hugged her a lot, but said nothing.

At the time, she had thought that he was being careful. After being hurt by one relationship, he hadn't wanted to get too deeply involved in another.

Now she thought different.

Bobby hadn't wanted to commit himself to her because it wasn't her that he wanted. It had been Laurie he'd loved all along, that's why he was continuing this ridiculous investigation. He had never got over Laurie; he had gone out with her because she was Laurie's best friend and in that way he could get back at his ex-girlfriend.

She reached her own front door. The hall light was on. Her dad was out. She sat down at the kitchen table, her jacket still on, her hands in her pockets as though she were cold and waiting for a bus on a chilly street corner.

There were some women who never let go of the men that they were involved with. Her mum, Laurie Drake. What was so special about them?

Jessie summoned up a picture of Laurie in her head. It was vague and blurred but she could see her old friend clearly enough. Short with shoulder-length dark brown hair, on her head was that floppy hat that she had bought at Oxfam. She was thin and flat-chested; it had always been something she had worried about. She had big feet as well, size sevens, so she could always pick up expensive shoes in half-price sales.

She was no beauty but the boys always liked her. She was chatty, could make them feel at ease after only a few moments in her company.

Jessie's dad had said that about her. She remembered an evening during the time that her dad was "recovering" from her mum's departure, when he'd just returned after dropping Laurie off home, he'd said, "Your friend Laurie has a way of talking that makes you feel relaxed. You forget sometimes that she's only a kid. It's like talking to another adult."

"Charming!" Jessie had said. "We are adults, almost!"

"You know what I mean . . ." her dad had said, biting his thumbnail. Jessie had looked at him and felt a stab of anxiety. Since her mum had left he'd become childlike.

Her mum. Jessie got up and took her coat off and hung it over the back of one of the kitchen chairs.

Her dad had never got over her mum. Once or twice lately he'd called her by her mum's name. He'd laughed it off but she could see that it had upset him.

She remembered the blue letter that he had been looking at the previous day. She wondered what it had said, whether it was one of the little "wooden" messages, that gave a new address and hoped that he was well; or the letters that arose from guilt where her mum would try, for the umpteenth time to explain to her dad why she had left.

Jessie looked around the room. She wanted to read it. She wanted to know what her mum was saying, what excuses she was making this time.

She opened the kitchen drawers and rifled through the piles of booklets and odds and ends. She looked on the shelves, in between the cookery books, where they sometimes wedged letters. She looked around the area of the phone, underneath the various pads and inside the address book.

Her dad must have put the letter away, in his desk. She looked at her watch. It was twenty past nine.

She wondered what Bobby was doing. Was he embarrassed, angry with her? She pictured the note with the newspaper letters on it, lying on the unit where she had left it. *FIND THE MAN SHE WAS INVOLVED WITH. HE IS RESPONSIBLE FOR HER DEATH.*

What did it all mean?

Her dad's desk was covered in files and bits of paper. The rest of his room was neat and tidy though and there was the faint smell of the aftershave that he had put on to go out. On the bed was a bright silk tie that he must have tried on and rejected before leaving. She picked it up for a moment.

Bobby Mathews never wore a tie, at least she had never seen him wear one. She wondered if he was phoning Anne, his new girlfriend. Was he telling her what had happened that evening? Were they both laughing at her expense?

She felt her throat drying and swallowed a few times. This wasn't the time to start crying.

She stood up and rubbed her hands together and looked at the desk. It would take some time to find anything in that mess.

On the floor beside her were the piles of papers and files, just as they had been. That way she would know where to replace them all, so that her dad wouldn't know that she had been searching for anything.

There was no sign of the blue letter. Maybe he had thrown it away. Maybe he had been angry with its contents and chucked it in the nearest bin.

She began to open the drawers. They were full of pens and felt-tips and old school diaries. There was a drawer full of running magazines and in another drawer was her dad's Walkman that he often used while he was marking books.

The bottom drawer on the left had a pile of holiday brochures in and she was about to close it when she saw a small flowered box in the back. She pulled the drawer out as far as it would go and reached in to take it out.

It was the size of a small shoe box. It was cardboard but covered with fabric and on the top was a tassel for taking the lid off.

Jessie recognized it immediately. It had been her mother's. She'd used it to keep receipts in and sometimes, when they were returning something to a shop, she would tell Jessie to get it down from the top of her wardrobe and painstakingly search through for the relevant bit of paper.

Her mum had left the box behind when she left them. Now her dad used it for his odds and ends.

Jessie took the lid off.

In the box were some small photographs and some letters in blue envelopes. She picked up the top one. It had the most recent postmark. She was about to open it when she noticed, in the corner of the photograph underneath, a face that she knew.

She took the photograph out.

It was a picture of Laurie Drake. She was leaning against a car and waving at the camera.

Jessie held it in her hand for a few moments. She looked at the box and then the drawer, as if to check that that was really where she found it.

On the back there was some writing.

You're not such an old man after all!
Much love, Laurie xxx

She turned the photograph back over and looked closely at it, as though she might have made a mistake, as though it wasn't really her Laurie, but another Laurie that her dad had a photograph of.

It was Laurie Drake though and the car that she was leaning against was her dad's car.

There was no mistaking it.

On the back were three kisses.

Kisses for her dad.

11

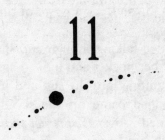

"Can I speak to Bobby Mathews, please?" Jessie played nervously with the phone flex as she waited for Bobby to come to the phone. She could hear the TV set from the living-room and the sounds of a newspaper turning.

"Bobby, it's Jessie—" She stopped because he had started speaking as soon as he heard her voice.

"No, look, it's me who should apologize," she said. "I just got carried away, but anyway that's not what I rang you for." She stood silently for a few seconds, allowing him to speak.

"It's nice of you to say that, Bobby, but it was a silly thing to do and I'm sorry. Anyway the point is, about Laurie." In the back pocket of her jeans she could feel the stiffness of the photograph of Laurie, leaning up against her dad's car. "The thing is I don't want to be involved in your . . ." For a moment she didn't know what to call it. Investigation? Enquiry? "I think I'd just rather drop this thing about Laurie's death." She patted her jeans pocket, "I think it's a waste of time as well as being upsetting."

He continued talking though and she pulled the photo out of her pocket and looked again. Laurie's eyes were squinting into the sun and Jessie noticed that her top had come off the shoulder on one side. She turned it over. *You're not such an old man after all! Much love Laurie xxx.*

"I don't know about the note. Maybe you should take it to the . . ." She was about to say the police but stopped. She rubbed the glossy photo with her finger and thumb and let him speak. In the end she just said, "I've got to go Bobby, I'm sorry."

She could still hear his voice as she replaced the receiver. She put the photo back into her jeans pocket just as the living-room door opened and her dad came out.

"Hello love," he said. "Who are you phoning?"

"It's private," she said sharply and watched her father's face flinch as though her words had hit him.

She turned and walked up the stairs. Why should she tell him everything about her life?

He had kept his affair with Laurie secret from her, why shouldn't she have some secrets?

12

Lesley Bradley's house faced onto the park. Jessie had visited her there with the others a couple of times. Laurie had gone more often, had baby-sat on a few occasions.

Jessie hadn't felt like going at all that afternoon. She hadn't felt like a nice chat about old times, about Laurie, about her own future. Her dad had annoyed her that morning when she'd told him she was going.

"Maybe she'll give you some advice, about the future," he'd said tentatively, probably aware that she was angry with him about something.

"I don't need any advice, from her or anyone." She'd said it softly but it had sounded hard and he had turned away and walked into the kitchen.

She'd been saying those kind of things all weekend, ever since she'd found the photo of Laurie in his secret box. The words had just shot out of her mouth at various times and he had been wounded, she had known.

He'd said nothing though, had taken it all silently. Jessie had wanted him to get angry with her, to retort, but he hadn't. His shoulders had just dropped a little and he'd bitten his thumbnail or fidgeted with whatever was in his hand. Perhaps that's what had driven her mum so mad, his unwillingness to talk, to ask her what was wrong. Her mum had left *him*, after all.

But then he'd had Laurie, her best friend. Laurie and he behind everyone's back, laughing and joking. You're not such an old man after all, she had said. No need to be an Einstein to work out what that meant.

Laurie had liked her dad a lot. Jessie stood at Lesley Bradley's wrought-iron gate and remembered her saying, "Your dad's so nice, so easy to talk to."

But then Laurie always got on well with older people.

Jessie rang the doorbell and turned to gaze through the giant trees that stood guard around the edge of the park. Laurie was always raving about Lesley Bradley and her wonderful house.

"It was a shell when they bought it. They've

restored it back to the way it was when it was first built. They've even found old leaded glass to go in the windows!''

"Does that mean there's no central heating or hot water and it's lit with gas?" Dodger had said when she'd been telling them.

"No, silly, you know what I mean." Laurie had given Dodger a cold look and turned away.

Jessie rang the bell again and looked at the leaded glass in the windows of the door. It had been beautifully done. Then it opened and she was faced with a man in running gear, taller than her dad, but adjusting his watch in the same way that he did before a run.

"Hello. Jessica, isn't it?" he said, concentrating on his watch. "Lesley," he shouted. "Jessica is here." And then he walked past her out of the front door.

Lesley came down the stairs with a baby in her arms. On the floor of the hall, in the middle of a small construction of Lego bricks sat the other child.

"I'm not too early am I?" Jessie said, feeling strange, awkward. She smiled and stepped across the toddler.

"No, I'm just making some tea," Lesley said, walking off into the kitchen. The small child was craning its head over her shoulder to have a look at Jessie. Lesley stopped for a moment and whispered something to the child. Then she turned and said, "Earl Grey or Lapsang Souchong?"

"I don't mind," Jessie said. Posh tea! She pursed her lips at a memory and walked into the big kitchen.

The first time they had all been to Lesley Bradley's house was at the beginning of the winter term, just after Christmas. Lesley had invited all her tutor group to come for Sunday afternoon tea. She and Laurie hadn't known what to make of the invitation. Sunday tea sounded so formal, like something her grandmother might have done when she was a young woman.

In the end, about ten of them had turned up, the rest making plausible excuses about illness or other commitments. They'd all sat in a long kitchen-dining room at the back of the house. The floor-boards had been stripped and there were house plants on every available surface. In the middle was a huge wooden table which had been laid out with china cups and saucers and side plates. There were larger plates of sandwiches and a silver platter covered wih slices of dark fruit cake.

"Would you like Earl Grey or Lapsang Souchong?" Lesley had said holding a delicate teapot in each hand. A few of them had murmured assent and held out their cups, but Dodger had nudged Jessie in the ribs and said, "Lapsang who?"

Bobby and Laurie had been sitting together a

few feet away and Jessie had caught Bobby's eye just as Dodger had made his comment.

"It's posh tea you berk,' Bobby had snapped and there was silence for a few seconds while Dodger just stared back at him. Jessie heard someone's spoon clink and somebody else saying, "What's that brown cake with the bits in?"

"It's china tea," Jessie said, nudging Dodger and smiling across at Bobby, trying to lighten the atmosphere.

One of the other kids, unaware of the tension, shouted from the other end of the table, "Dodge thought it was something you could get from a Chinese takeaway!" and a few people had laughed.

Jessie had felt Dodger's small body stiffen on the chair next to her. She'd put her hand on his arm and looked at Laurie for support. Laurie and Bobby were talking quietly, though looking into the pale cream teacup in front of them, oblivious of Dodger's discomfort.

Suddenly Dodger had laughed out loud. "A portion of fried rice and Lapsangsou," he'd said, and held his cup out to Lesley Bradley.

She'd sighed exaggeratedly and poured tea into the tiny cup. Dodger had drunk his tea and eaten a piece of fruit cake then left. He'd been smiling and making jokes but Jessie had known he was unhappy, that he'd been hurt. She should have gone after him, but Laurie and Bobby had started a game of charades and she'd wanted to stay.

"I was never clear why you decided to put off going to university," Lesley Bradley said, taking a sip from a pale pink mug of tea.

"Oh, you know," Jessie started, "I had some problems at home, you know my mum and dad separated and what with Laurie and stuff nothing seemed very clear." Jessie looked at the small child strapped in the high chair opposite. "How old is she?" she said.

"Don't try and change the subject," Lesley said, adopting her register-taking tone of voice. "I know you've had some problems and I know how upset you were when Laurie committed suicide – we all were. But life has to go on. It's a cliché I know, but you can't afford to let things that are beyond your control run your life for you. Look at Bobby Mathews, it ruined his education, and Dodger; he was never the same."

Jessie nodded half-heartedly. Lesley had drifted into her counselling mode of speaking.

"It's just that—" she said and then she stopped. What could she say? She wasn't sure of anything any more. Why hadn't she gone to university? Because her dad would be alone? Because once her friend had died things like qualifications and degrees didn't seem to be worth a light? Because she knew then for definite she wouldn't see Bobby

Mathews? "I thought I'd have a year off to think about it. I've got a place next year at Canterbury." She was about to say that she was saving money and was going to travel but the sound of a bell ringing stopped her.

"Oh," Lesley said. "It's probably Tom."

Jessie was relieved that their talk had been interrupted. She got up and picked up a small rattle that the baby had dropped and as Lesley and her husband came back into the room she was looking at some photographs that had been put in glass clip frames on the wall opposite.

"I'll take Sarah to the park, if you like, get her out of your way," Tom said.

"No, she's playing good as gold."

The couple were talking quietly and Jessie concentrated on the photos. She wondered how long before she could politely leave.

"Do you want me to look after Emma?"

"No, you chat to Jessica, while I put her upstairs for a nap."

Jessie closed her eyes with irritation. She wished she hadn't come. She hated being "looked after" as though she was a small child who had to be entertained. She felt Tom's footsteps approaching and jumped into the conversation first.

"Did you win?" she said, pointing to a photo of him among some other runners.

"No," he said. "Did a good time though," and

he carried on talking about distances, minutes and seconds. But Jessie had turned off. Whenever her dad started on about the intricate details of running she usually adopted a glazed look and thought of other things.

"Where is this?" Jessie pointed to another photo in which Tom was standing in front of a tiny tent on the side of a hill. There was a light covering of snow on the ground and on the tent. Tom was dressed as though he was off on an expedition to the Antarctic.

"Survival training," he said. "Me and a mate spend some time each year fending for ourselves in Wales. No modern amenities."

"Back to nature," Lesley said, walking into the kitchen, followed by the older child.

"Oh," Jessie said. She looked at her watch. "I'll have to make a move. My dad runs," she said as an afterthought. "Mostly half marathons. He's never managed a full one."

"Tom does a couple of those every summer. We usually plan our holidays around them. Men!" Lesley rolled her eyes and laughed. Jessie was thinking about going back home though, facing her dad. Maybe she should have it out with him, show him the photo, tell him she knew.

Lesley gave her her jacket and she put it on as she walked along the hallway.

"I've seen Dodger from time to time. Perhaps

you could come to supper together one night. I always thought you and he got on quite well." Lesley Bradley was adopting a matchmaking tone of voice.

Jessie said, "Um . . ." and looked away from her old teacher as she opened the front door. She noticed, to her right, the wall was covered in advertisements for exhibitions of artists. The Tate Gallery, the National Gallery. They were bold and yet intricate and Jessie remembered studying similar ones in her Communications A level.

"Those are striking," she said, glad to change the subject.

"Tom's the art lover," Lesley said. "Look, sorry we didn't have long to talk. You must come again, when you've made some decisions. I might be able to help."

"I will," Jessica said. But when she walked out of the wrought-iron gate into the street she knew that she never would.

13

There were hardly any people in the park and Jessie sat on a bench for a while to watch a small child and its mother feeding some heavy-looking ducks by the side of a small pond.

The child was throwing wedges of bread at the ducks and squealing with pleasure as they took it in their flat beaks and waddled back off towards the water.

If Laurie had lived and had her baby then it would be about three or four months old by now. Was it her dad's baby? It if had been her dad's baby would that mean it would have been her half-brother or sister? Would Laurie have got married to her dad and been her step-mother?

Jessie smiled at the ridiculousness of it. Had her

dad really been involved with Laurie? What was her evidence? She sat back and watched the mum and toddler walk off towards the swings. She was beginning to sound like Bobby Mathews. Evidence! It was his stupid theory that had got her into this. If he hadn't started all this she wouldn't be in this position now.

All he really had was a theory and an anonymous note that didn't really tell him anything.

All she had was a photo with a message on the back. By itself it didn't add up to much. What made it suspicious was the fact that her dad had kept it hidden away in a drawer in his desk as though he didn't want it to be found. Jessie had racked her brain thinking back over those months leading up to the summer holidays when Laurie disappeared off to Cromer. She tried to pinpoint times when her dad had gone out for days or evenings when she hadn't seen Laurie but nothing stood out. It was all a blur. When Laurie had gone off to Cromer her dad hadn't seemed upset. He'd just continued his training for the Norwich half marathon. He'd been at home every day, painting the outside of the house, running for hours, taking long showers and reading books.

The only time he'd gone away was with the running club to Norwich.

Norwich.

Jessie sat up, feeling uncomfortable. She pulled

her jacket tightly round her. Her dad had spent four or five days in Norwich, staying with some friends from another club.

Norwich was in Norfolk and so was Cromer.

Jessie stood up and started to walk out of the park, towards home. There was nothing else for it. She would have to speak to him, show him the photo, find out what had happened between them.

Not that she thought for a minute that her dad might have been the person that Bobby thought was a murderer. She didn't go along with that theory. It was full of holes.

But what about the note? *FIND THE MAN SHE WAS INVOLVED WITH. HE IS RESPONSIBLE FOR HER DEATH.*

If her dad had been involved with Laurie and afraid that people would find out – afraid that she would find out – might that not have made him break it off? Tell Laurie that it was finished?

Could that have been why Laurie killed herself?

Her strides became longer as she neared her street. It wasn't murder though, not what Bobby thought. But what if it had been her dad who *caused* Laurie to kill herself?

Laurie in her beat-up mini, driving into Epping Forest, parking in a lonely lane, her car hidden by bushes and trees, a bottle of wine and some tablets on the seat beside her. A child's toy that she usually carried when she wanted good luck.

Jessie stopped and leant against a wall. In the back of her head she could hear a siren from an ambulance or a police car. It was in the distance but sounded cross and bad-tempered. Her dad could have been responsible for Laurie's death. He might not have killed her like Bobby thought, but he might have pushed her over the edge.

She began to walk again, turning the corner into her street. She'd ask him about Laurie as soon as she got in. That way it would be cleared up once and for all.

She stopped after a few steps though and looked at the police car parked outside her house. A feeling of nausea rose like a hiccup in her throat and she walked on up her path and opened the front door with a shaking hand.

14

She could hear her dad's voice from the living-room. Inside her head she had a picture of him sitting, his face ashen, his hands rubbing together as though he was cold. The policeman would have a notebook open and would be on the brink of reading him his rights.

"You have the right to remain silent . . ."

But when she steeled herself and opened the door all she could see was a WPC standing by the mantelpiece, a china cup and saucer in her hand. Relief hit her like a warm gust, but she stiffened again when she saw Bobby Mathews sitting on the settee.

"Bobby?" she said.

"Jessie, love." Her dad stood up. "Bobby has

brought WPC Williams here to talk about Laurie Drake's death."

"Please call me Joan," the WPC said.

"Why?" Jessie said, an image of Laurie leaning on her dad's car in her head.

"There has been a development," the policewoman said. "I believe you already know about the first note."

"Why didn't you tell me about all this, Jessie?" her dad said.

"I . . . I . . ." Jessie looked from one to the other. On the table was an envelope file of Bobby's. It probably held his theory and the new anonymous letter that might implicate her dad.

"Jessie, I couldn't keep quiet about it. There's been another letter."

"Another letter?" Jessie felt weak. She put her hand over her mouth.

"She's upset," the WPC said. "Laurie was her friend after all."

Jessie swallowed hard. In a minute Bobby or the WPC would take out the second note. She would have to read it, knowing more than they did about the older man that Laurie was involved with. She reached out for the arm of the chair and sat down.

"I'll get her a cup of tea," her dad said. Bobby came over to her and grabbed her hand.

"It's all right, Jessie. I'm sure we'll get somewhere with this note. We're closing in on him."

He handed her the piece of paper. It was as before, with words from a newspaper stuck haphazardly across the page. *We're closing in on him!* Bobby was still thinking of himself as a character in a detective film. He didn't realize how serious all this digging around was, what sort of secrets it was going to uproot.

She could hear the WPC talking to her dad as she looked at the note. "Is there any more tea, Mr Morris?"

"Call me Terry, please."

The paper had been roughly torn out of an exercise book, its edges were wavy and in one corner it was wrinkled. On it were the words, *ASK THEM ABOUT LAURIE IN CROMER. THEN YOU'LL FIND OUT ABOUT HER BOYFRIEND. HE IS RESPONSIBLE FOR HER DEATH.*

Cromer. How far was Cromer from Norwich?

Close enough, Jessie thought, closing her eyes.

"Look Jessica," the WPC said, "we're going to get out the files and just look over the evidence to see if any of the points that Bobby has made are worth looking into."

"Like the fact that there was no container for the sleeping tablets and the lucky mascot that she had with her," Bobby said, counting the points off on his fingers.

"Yes, yes, we will examine these things but, as I've said to Bobby, all this was carefully looked into at the time. The officers who handled the case were convinced that it was suicide."

"What about the mystery lover?" Bobby said, beginning to look a bit peeved.

Jessie looked over at her dad to catch his eyes, to see if he registered anything. But he was looking at the WPC.

"Maybe she was involved with someone else, that we don't know. What we do know is there was no one in the car with her when she died."

"And these?" Jessie picked the letter up off the table.

"Who knows? It could be some friend of hers, someone who wants to cause a bit of mischief."

Jessie sat back, the cup of tea in her hand untouched. The WPC put her hat back on.

"Tell her about what Dodger said." Bobby looked straight at Jessie.

"Well . . ." she frowned. Why had he brought that into it? That wasn't evidence, that was just Dodger.

"It's OK Bobby," the WPC said, "I've written all that down. I promise you I will look into it. If anything comes up I'll be in touch."

"I'll show you out, Officer," her dad said.

"Please, call me Joan."

Bobby stood for a moment and Jessie looked

him up and down. This was all his fault, all because he couldn't let go of Laurie.

"What do you want now?" She said it harshly.

"Do you fancy a walk, down by the river? We could go over all this," he said, raising his envelope file, a half smile on his lips.

He had such charm, that was the trouble. Inside her there was a voice that was urging her to go, just to be with him. It didn't matter what they talked about.

But in her back pocket was the photo of Laurie leaning against her dad's car.

"No thanks," she said. "I've got something I've got to do."

15

When she heard the front door slam Jessie took the photo out of her pocket and laid it flat on the table in front of her.

Her dad came back into the room. "Jessie, I wish you had said something about all this to me—"

He stopped still, looking at the photo. "Where did you get that? Have you been looking through my things?"

He picked it up and she was about to speak, to ask him about it, when he threw it back onto the table. "You have no right to go through my things. This is private. It's nobody's business but mine. You have no right. Can you imagine—"

"Dad . . ."

"Can you imagine how you would feel if it had been the other way round? If I had gone through your things?"

"Dad . . ." she said, shocked by his righteousness, his anger. It should have been the other way round. She should have been angry with him.

"You've got no bloody right!" he said and walked out of the room.

Later she went up to his bedroom and knocked on the door.

"Are you decent?" she said, her voice light.

"Yes."

"Can I come in?"

She sat on the edge of his bed, the photo in her hand. He was in his running gear, sorting through the drawer for socks.

"I didn't deliberately go through your things. I was looking for my birth certificate, to get my passport sorted out." She'd decided to lie about it. "I thought it might be in one of the files in your desk. I found the box. I recognized it. It used to be Mum's." She stopped for a minute. Her dad started to pull the laces out of a pair of trainers that were on the floor. "I found this accidentally. I . . . we . . . me and Bobby have been thinking about Laurie's death. He's convinced she was involved with some older bloke, someone who wouldn't have wanted anyone to find out about their affair."

Her dad was concentrating on the laces, ripping them out of each eyelet until they were hanging long and wrinkled over his hand.

"Go on," he said, without looking up.

"Why do you think I've been so upset all weekend?"

"What conclusion did you come to?" he said.

"I don't know. I remember how much Laurie liked you, she was always saying nice things, I thought . . ."

"You thought that I was the older man. Laurie's secret lover. The one who Bobby Mathews thinks knows about her death."

"Maybe. I don't know. The message on the back . . ."

Her dad sat back. He dropped the unlaced trainer on to the floor and raised his feet one by one to put on some sports socks. When he'd finished he sat and looked at her for a moment and Jessie didn't know what to say. His expression was unreadable. She didn't know if he was angry or not. His lips looked as though they might be on the verge of a smile but his eyebrows were pursed. For those few moments he didn't look like her dad at all.

Then he started to chuckle softly. "So you thought you'd be Sherlock Holmes and try to find out what happened between Laurie and me."

Jessie forced her lips into a smile. He was making fun of her.

"Do you blame me for thinking that?" she said.

"Yes," he said. "I thought you knew me better than that."

They sat for a while in silence, her dad re-threading the trainer lace, she rubbing her thumb against the glossy surface of the photograph. Finally he said, "It was round about Easter, in the school holidays, I was here marking books – your mum was long gone by then, living with lover-boy. Laurie came round just before lunch to see you. I forget where you were, shopping I think or at some museum in London with some other pals.

"It was one of those early spring days, you know, everyone walking round in their shirtsleeves, their heavy winter coats over their arms, just in case. She was at a loose end, she said. She suggested going for a pub lunch up in Epping Forest somewhere.

"I just said yes. I didn't think about what it would look like. As far as I was concerned she was a friend of the family. I didn't think of her as a potential girlfriend, she was just a companion, someone to spend an afternoon with.

We went to that pub up at High Beech, you know, the one with the big garden. We had a couple of halves and a sandwich and then she suggested going for a walk. She had her camera in her bag and wanted to take some photos. I should've realized then that it hadn't been one of those last minute ideas. Why on earth would she have her camera with her? But I didn't think. We went walking. It was a glorious afternoon, warm enough to sunbathe in.

"We sat in a sunny spot and chatted. She was a bright girl, could hold her end of the conversation up. I remember she started talking about Shakespeare and her favourite play, *Romeo and Juliet*. She started quoting bits from it." Her dad stopped talking and reached for his second trainer.

"She just started kissing me. I know that sounds ridiculous and I should have stopped her. I'm a grown man, she was a young girl, my daughter's friend.

"But it was hot and we'd had a drink. She'd been chatting away so confidently that I'd almost forgotten who she was, how old she was. We kissed for a while and I kept ignoring that nagging little voice in my head that said, 'What the hell are you doing?'

"We got back to the car and she wanted me to take a photo of her. As we were driving back I began to realize what an idiot I'd been. Me, a school teacher, kissing a seventeen-year-old girl in Epping Forest, my daughter's friend. I dropped her off at her house without saying anything and when I got back home you were in. I don't think I've ever done such a thoughtless, dangerous thing."

He tied his trainer up and got up and went across to the desk. He picked up a black watch and put it on his wrist.

"Over the next couple of days I guess I just hoped that she'd sort of forget it, ridiculous as that sounds. She didn't though. She rang me a couple of times. It was laughable really; she'd start by saying, 'Are you alone? Is Jessie around?' You know, as if you were my wife and I was having an affair with her.

"I kept thinking, it was only a few kisses, nothing else. The trouble was she was more serious. She came round here one evening when you were at some college do and said that she loved me. She gave me the photo."

"What did you do?" Jessie said.

"I was pretty horrible to her. I knew there was no point in letting her down gently. I reminded her that she had a boyfriend, that I was old enough to be her father, et cetera. In the end I just told her that she wasn't my type. Too immature; she had too much growing up to do. I had to be hard. She was arguing with every objection I made. I had to be cruel, to make her realize that it was completely out of the question.

"She went home in tears. I thought she might tell you; I was in nerves for days. I should've thrown the photo away really, but I was sort of touched. In some ways it shocked me out of mooning over Mum. I managed to avoid her for a few weeks. Then, when I did see her again, she was friendly enough, but reserved."

Her dad stood in front of her, ready for his run. For a moment she was reminded of the photo of Lesley Bradley's husband, the same kind of T-shirt and tight-fitting shorts.

"I'm off now," he said. "Sorry I've mucked up your theory. Anyway, I couldn't keep hold of your mother, so what chance would I have courting a teenager?" He went out of the bedroom laughing quietly to himself.

Courting. It was a funny old-fashioned word. It was the dating stage, where young people went out places together, like she and Bobby had done, although they hadn't called it that.

She looked at the photo. Laurie Drake and her father. What would she have felt like if she had known that Laurie was trying to seduce her dad?

She lay back on her dad's bed. His bedside clock said five forty-nine. She'd been wrong about everything. Wrong about Laurie, Bobby, and now wrong about her dad. She had all but accused him of something he hadn't done.

She thought of the police woman and her assumption that she had come to arrest her dad! It was all a mixed-up mess.

She sat up. But the anonymous letters were being sent by someone. And the last one said, *ASK ABOUT LAURIE IN CROMER*.

There was something funny about it all. Then she remembered Dodger. *I celebrated when she died.*

And the lucky troll. Why would she bring that if she was going to kill herself?

She got up and put her shoes back on. She couldn't leave things as they were. It was as if they'd opened up Laurie's life and were finding horrible things there. They had to put it right.

Half an hour later she walked up to Bobby's front door. He opened it. She took a deep breath and said, "Bobby, let's go to Cromer next weekend. Let's see what we can find out about Laurie."

"What?"

"It doesn't matter what's changed my mind. I think we should clear this thing up once and for all. Shake on it?" She held her hand out and he looked at her for a few seconds. Then he took her hand in both of his and held it tightly.

"Cromer it is," he said.

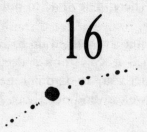

16

On Friday morning Jessie was at the super-market packing shelves with pasta and sauces: lasagne, fusilli, penne and tagliatelle.

In her head she had a mental list and she was ticking off the Things To Do about the trip to Cromer.

She'd already told her dad she was staying with a friend from work. She'd booked two single rooms in the Seaview B&B in Cromer. All she had to do was get two weekend return train tickets.

She began to sort the jars of sauces: bolognese, napoletana, pesto, carbonara. A woman came up and asked her where the sun-dried tomatoes were. She smiled and pointed to them.

She felt relaxed and hopeful. The tension about

her and Bobby, about her dad and Laurie had gone. Her shoulders and the back of her neck had felt rigid, frozen; now the worry had melted. It was no longer important if Bobby still wanted her or not. Her dad wasn't the mystery lover who had been involved in Laurie's death.

A small child rushed across the aisle into her legs and fell over. She crouched down and helped her up.

"There, there," she said. The child's mother scooped the little girl up and rolled her eyes at Jessie.

"I'm so sorry," she said above the child's cries.

"It's OK," Jessie said, raising her voice.

"You're in a good mood today," her friend Sarah said. She was wheeling a trolley full of tins of cat food.

"Yes, I suppose I am."

She had to sort out the questions about Laurie's death, to forget about what happened between her and Bobby Mathews. That was all over. She took a deep breath. She said it to herself, 'It's all over between me and Bobby Mathews'. She waited for a few seconds for the awful crumpling feeling in her stomach that usually accompanied thoughts like this. In her hand was a tin of cooking sauce which she placed slowly onto the shelf. There was nothing. She began to breathe more easily and looked at her watch. It was ten thirty.

This time tomorrow we'll be on the train, she thought.

She was on the till when she saw Dodger wandering up an aisle towards her. He had a basket over his arm which had a couple of shopping items in it. As he came closer she saw that he looked just as unkempt as he had the last time she had seen him. His jacket was wrinkled and looked as though it had been slept in, his hair looked greasy and there was a tuft sticking bolt upright on the top of his head where it hadn't been combed. He waited in line behind a man who was unloading his shopping.

When she finally got to him she said, "How are you, Dodge?"

"Exceptionally well, young lady," he said and grinned. For a brief moment Jessie had an image of him in his college days, well-dressed, full of charm and wit. Then she looked at his trembling hand unloading his basket: two four-packs of strong lager.

"Where are you living?" she said, packing his lager cans into a carrier bag.

He laughed. "I have a little pad down by the river. Come and see! Come for lunch! I have the beverages."

"I'm a bit busy . . ." she started to say. She'd wanted to go and book the train tickets for the journey to Cromer.

"Of course you are. Busy busy bee. And, anyway, why would you want to come and see me? You and Laurie Drake, always so busy."

"Dodger!" she said, her anger rising. She pulled a piece of paper off the till roll and shoved it at him. She got her pen out of her top pocket.

"Write down the address. I'll be there at one. You and me have got to sort out some stuff about Laurie, once and for all."

"Address?" he said, laughing. "Just go to the old community centre. I'll see you there, providing I don't get a better offer."

She got to the old community centre about one fifteen. It was closed up with strips of wood nailed across the windows. The sign across the door was still there, "Riverside Community Centre, opened June 1972".

There were still some yellowing posters stuck on the wood that said, Save Our Community Centre and Stop the Cuts.

Jessie looked for some sign of entry, a door or a window, there was none. She walked round to the side of the building. In the distance she could hear reggae music, the kind that Dodger liked. It was low and tinny. She called out, "Dodger?"

A moment later he was standing in front of her.

"Welcome," he said with his arms open in an exaggerated gesture, "to my humble abode." He dropped one arm but the other stayed up and pointed to a back door that was open.

"Let's go in, shall we?" he said.

"Is this where you *live*?" Jessie looked around the darkened room that had previously been an office. The window had been boarded up but there were cracks of light coming through where the planks of wood didn't quite meet. In one corner there was an old desk that still had a blotting pad on it. There were piles of old newspapers scattered across it. By its side was a brown cupboard, the door of which was hanging on one set of hinges. On one wall were a couple of curling posters for sunny holidays. Come to Barbados. Discover Spain.

In a corner, over by the window, were a couple of sleeping-bags and some cardboard boxes. There was a small Primus stove, a tin kettle and a cassette player.

"All mod cons," Dodger said. "There's even a lock on the door for absolute privacy, see?" Dodger turned a key in a rusted lock.

"You *live* here?" she said again.

Dodger stiffened. "Believe me, Jess, it's better than shop doorways. Me and a couple of lads found it a week or so ago. One bloke, used to be a plumber, he turned the water on for us. All we need now is an electrician. Come and sit down," he said pointing to the sleeping-bag. "No bugs, I promise."

*　　*　　*

They were eating sandwiches that she had brought from the shop. Dodger had opened a can of the lager and was drinking it in great gulps. Jessie looked at her watch, she had about twenty minutes before she had to be back at work. She decided to be direct.

"Dodger why do you hate Laurie so much?" She said it gently and he continued to eat.

Eventually he put the can down and said, "Jess I don't hate Laurie at all. I loved Laurie, that was my problem. I loved her."

It was ten past two; she should have been back at work. Dodger was talking though and she couldn't leave.

"When I got the job in Cromer I thought we'd get together. She was fed up with Mathews. She'd told me she was going to finish with him. We hung around together for the first few weeks, she seemed happy to be with me. She had that way, you know, of touching my arm gently or giving me a quick hug at the end of the day.

"One night, after we'd been there a couple of weeks, she came to my room and stayed. We didn't do anything – except for a kiss or two – but she lay on my bed beside me. I remember I had one arm underneath her that had gone to sleep but I didn't move it. I was afraid that she would wake up and go."

Dodger stopped and pulled open another can of lager.

"After that night I thought it would only be a matter of time. She changed though."

"Changed?"

"Yes. There was this guy in the camp, a real body-beautiful, ex-army type. A lot of the girls liked him. Laurie started to talk about him all the time. Tim this, Tim that. He was married, he lived off-site, in Cromer itself.

"She disappeared off the camp one weekend. Someone said she was with him, camping. She seemed besotted. I couldn't get a serious word out of her.

"When we came back to London I thought she'd get over it, but she just got worse. She kept talking about her *true* love, the weekend in the forest, watching him run in some race in Norwich. It made me sick in the end."

The word Norwich made Jessie stiffen. Her dad ran in the half marathon there. Her thoughts were broken by a voice.

"Trevor, Trev, let me in," from outside the window.

"It's Billy," Dodger said, "me mate." He went out of the room and came back in with a kid who looked no more than about fourteen.

"I got these from the newsagents down near the station. He had his back to me and I just lifted them and walked away." He was carrying a pile of daily newspapers, the *Independent*, *The Times*, the *Guardian*.

"We only read the qualities," Dodger said.

They were standing on the street, outside the community centre.

"Me and Bobby Mathews are going to Cromer this weekend to find out anything we can about Laurie's time there." She didn't want to explain about the anonymous letters or the theory that Bobby had. In her head she couldn't help thinking about the Norwich half marathon and her dad. Had he lied to her?

Dodger's eyes were wandering across the road. He suddenly said, "You know, the night Laurie died I was down at Murphy's. Anyone will tell you that."

"OK," she said. It had been a funny thing to say and she felt a stab of pity for him. She felt she ought to touch his arm or kiss him goodbye; she had no idea when they might meet again. But she didn't. She opened her bag and got a five pound note out.

"Dodge, here . . ." She offered the money.

Dodger just looked at it.

"Put your money away. There are better charities around than me. Anyway, this is all temporary. I've got plans. Do me one favour though."

"What?" she asked, the crumpled five pound note in a little ball in her hand.

"Don't call me Dodger now. The name's Trevor, or Trev to my special friends."

17

When they got off the train at Cromer the wind hit them in short blasts. They had their tickets checked and asked for directions to "Seaview".

Jessie was carrying a small rucksack on her back, her head down, her shoulders into the wind. Bobby Mathews had a small holdall and had the palm of his hand across his face to stop bits of paper or dirt hitting him in the eye.

They left their belongings in the guest house and went to a tea shop on the front that was still open.

"How far is the camp?" Bobby asked, cupping a hot mug of tea in his hands.

"A couple of kilometres outside Cromer, the man said." Jessie was gazing out of the window.

The sea was brown and frothy and the sky was creamy. The wind, like an invisible hand, was pulling people's coats and playing with their hair. There was a couple on the beach throwing bits of wood to a black and white dog who kept running in the opposite direction. The woman kept standing still, her hands on her hips while the man appeared to be laughing.

"We could walk it," Bobby said, looking into his cup of tea.

"I suppose so," she said, looking at a boat in the distance.

"Um . . ." he said and fell into silence.

Jessie sighed. It was awkward between them. It had been since she'd told him all the things that Dodger had said.

Bobby had listened in silence, his face expressionless. Now and then he'd closed his eyes and kept them shut for a few seconds. Finally he'd said, "I knew he liked her but I never realized how much. She was that sort of person, you see. When she first knew you she sort of took over your life. She'd ring me every day and do things for me, like photocopy notes of lectures that I missed or go all the way up to Oxford Street to get me a special CD that I wanted."

Jessie had nodded. She knew what he meant. When she had first made friends with Laurie it had been like that. They went out together all the time and often ate round each other's houses. If they had a day at college when they didn't see much of each other she would get a phone call in the evening from Laurie asking her what she was up to.

When her mum left Laurie had been tremendous. Looking back now Jessie gave a wry smile. Had she fancied her dad right from the start?

Bit by bit she had drifted away though. Jessie had put it down to her involvement with Bobby Mathews. She hadn't been hurt exactly; she hadn't taken it personally. Laurie was ready to move on; they were still friends as far as she was concerned.

Dodger had been hurt though; so had Bobby. What about the other man? The older mystery man? Did she hurt him or did he hurt her?

Now they were in Cromer and would probably find out more uncomfortable things about Laurie.

"We could get a mini cab," Bobby said eventually, pushing the empty mug away. His shoulders were rounded and his chin seemed to be resting on his chest. He had lost heart, it was clear. The whole weekend was going to be a failure. Maybe he was fed up with the whole thing and wanted to get back to his new girlfriend Anne.

"Look," she said in a businesslike way, "we're here to find out some things about Laurie. Those things might not be very nice but it's what we've come for. When we've found out what we want to know then we can both get on with our lives again. You and Anne and your dad's business; me saving up and going to university next year."

He began to smile. "What about Tony, your boyfriend?"

She ignored the comment and continued. "It's important to get this sorted out. I think we should find out the quickest way to the camp and get on."

"OK, boss," Bobby said and began to put his coat on.

As they walked out the door of the tea rooms he said, "By the way, me and Anne are finished."

By road the camp was three kilometres. Across country it was about one and a half kilometres.

"Just stick to the footpath indicated on the map," the man in the sweet shop said. The map had cost fifty pence and was a photocopy of a hand drawing by a local enthusiast. Down the side there were notes about the hedgerows and vegetation. Jessie read about them while she walked along. Bobby was a few metres in front.

"We've got to cross this stile and turn half right," she said when they came to the end of a field.

"Half right," Bobby said, "how can you turn half right?"

"Oh, you town dwellers!"

"Philip Marlowe never had to do this," Bobby said. Jessie noticed that his holdall had the corner of an envelope file poking out. He even had his notes with him.

"A week or so ago," Jessie said, catching up with him, "you told me your theory about Laurie's death. Now let me tell you mine."

"OK," he said and slowed his walking pace down.

"I think that Laurie came to summer camp at a bit of a loose end. She had more or less finished with you."

"Thanks," he said.

"You've got to face it, Bobby. I haven't come all this way for us to pretend to each other." She stopped. She'd never told Bobby about Laurie's involvement with her dad. She'd persuaded herself that it was brief and unimportant. The Norwich half marathon had been a concidence, she had decided. A coincidence.

"Anyway, this is what I think. Laurie got involved with this bloke, Tim somebody. He is married, maybe has kids. She thought that she could tempt him away from his wife, you know how much of a challenge that would have been for her."

"You make her sound like a real cow."

"We've got to face up to it, Bobby, she wasn't very nice sometimes. Look at how she treated you and Dodger."

"I know . . . but . . ."

"Anyway, she comes to London, still seeing this

guy occasionally. Maybe he comes to London or they meet halfway. The point is, he's happy to continue; he's got a wife and he's got a girlfriend. What more could he ask for?"

"And?"

"And she finds she's pregnant. He's not going to leave his wife and tells her to get an abortion. She flips and kills herself."

"Then why the good luck mascot? Where's the container for the sleeping pills? Who is sending the anonymous notes?"

"I don't know. Maybe someone from the camp wants to get this Tim someone into trouble, maybe another girl that he was involved with. The rest is circumstantial and doesn't add up to anything. My God," she said, laughing, "I'm beginning to sound like I'm working for the Metropolitan Police!"

They were walking alongside a stream and hidden from the wind for a while. According to the map they were close to the centre.

"Let me suggest one other possibility," Bobby said.

"OK."

"You remember the note? 'Remember what Juliet says. Farewell! God knows when we shall meet again. I love you Laurie.'"

"Yes?"

"Last week I said to you that it could have been any note, that she'd written to him anytime. You know, star-crossed lovers and all that. But now I've changed my mind. What if it was meant to be a double suicide? She was sitting in the passenger seat after all. What if they'd both gone there to commit suicide because they couldn't be together only he'd got cold feet and not gone through with it. The reference to *Romeo and Juliet* is apt. They both ended up dead."

"A double suicide," Jessie said, screwing her face up.

"Maybe his wife is sick or crippled or something and he can't leave her, but he can't live without Laurie."

"Maybe Laurie didn't mean to kill herself. Perhaps it was a cry for help."

"Then why park in the middle of nowhere to do it? Hide the car under bushes? No, there's something more to all this." Bobby stopped. Up ahead were some outbuildings and barns. To the side of one of them was a small van that had the words "Outdoor Pursuits" printed on the side.

"Here we are," Jessie said and walked ahead.

"I'm sorry we can't help you," the caretaker, George, said. "Only my guv'nor bought this operation at Easter. It's still called by the same name but it's owned by a different bloke. We use one or two of the old staff, but the guv'nor really wanted a clean sweep. Apart from that, most of the workers here are casuals, some passing through, some live locally. Quite a few of them got their money in their hand, if you get my meaning."

Jessie did get his meaning. She looked at Bobby who had given up listening and had gone to look at the notice-board.

"We haven't got any records of employment, they would have been taken by the old owners. Tim did you say? And you haven't a second name? Ex-Army? It doesn't ring any bells at all, my dear."

"Thanks anyway," Jessie said and walked over towards Bobby. "Looks like it was a waste of time."

"Not necessarily," he said, getting his pencil out of his pocket. "Look at this."

The notice-board was covered with fliers for pubs and snack bars and discos. There were advertisements for pony trekking, cycling and cliff walks. Bobby was pointing at a small piece of blue paper which was pinned on top of some others.

CROMER RUNNERS. BEGINNERS OR ADVANCED CATERED FOR: ALL WELCOME: GO TO 'THE SEAFRONT DELI' AND ASK FOR TIM FRIAR.

"Tim. Tim Friar," she said. "Let's go."

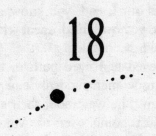

18

They got to the Seafront Deli about three o'clock. Bobby went in and Jessie followed. A man of about forty was serving a customer. When he'd finished Bobby said, "Is Tim Friar around?"

"Who wants to know?" the man said gruffly, putting the lid on a giant tub of coleslaw. Jessie noticed that he had a thin gold wedding ring on.

"We're . . ." Bobby turned back to Jessie and then continued, "we're friends of Laurie Drake. She used to work with him in the Outdoor Pursuits centre. We wanted to have a chat with him."

"Carry on then, I'm Tim Friar," he said and turned his back on them while he washed his hands.

Bobby was clearly disconcerted. He turned and

gave Jessie a puzzled look. Jessie thought he probably wasn't expecting someone so old. After she'd discovered about Laurie's feelings for her dad she was ready for anything. She took over. "Look, Tim, can we just talk to you for a while about Laurie? She was our friend, you know, and we just wanted to know how she'd spent the last few months of her life."

The man turned and eyed both of them suspiciously. A young woman suddenly emerged from a door behind him. She was about their age.

"Dad, I'm just going over to Mum's. I'll go straight to work from her house," she said, looking at Tim Friar with uncertainty.

"Make sure you come straight home after work." He mumbled the words and watched as the young girl went off through the same door. Jessie and Bobby looked at each other. Tim Friar had a daughter who was the same age as Laurie!

Then Bobby looked away and Jessie was left thinking about her own dad. He had kissed Laurie and yet he had a daughter of her age.

"You better come in the back," Tim Friar said, his face softening a bit.

"I hardly knew little Laurie," Tim Friar said, putting two cups of tea down on the kitchen table. "She hung around with all the young ones, as far as I knew. She came on a couple of staff meals and joined in with some of the camp activities. I thought she was close to that young man that she spent a lot of time with. Trevor someone."

Bobby and Jessie drank their tea in silence. Jessie sighed. The conversation was going nowhere. Every time they took a new turn they seemed to end at a brick wall.

"Apparently she went away for a weekend with a man," Bobby said, "and went to the Norwich half marathon to watch him run, we heard."

Tim Friar sat still for a moment. He had an apron on that had the words "Seafront Deli" written in large italics across his chest. His shoulders loomed out of each side of it making him look out of proportion. Jessie noticed that he had a hole in his ear where an earring had once been. Finally he said, "Now you mention it, she did come to the Norwich run. We gave her a lift, said she was seeing a friend. Yes, I remember now. She came with us, in the van and then when we got there she went off on her own."

"On her own?"

"Yeah. Said she had a friend from London to see. I saw her later with some older bloke, greying hair. They were kissing, as I remember. I had a joke with her afterwards. I remember now."

Jessie stiffened, her fingers glued to the handle of the cup.

"What was he like, isn't there anything else you

can remember about him?" Bobby said, sitting forward.

Tim Friar looked at him uneasily.

"Well, I don't rightly remember. Just tall, my height I suppose, dark brown hair with a lot of grey in it. Look," he raised his voice suddenly, "what is this? I thought you just wanted to chat about little Laurie and here you are cross-examining me!"

"No," Jessie said. "I'm sorry. You see, Laurie was pregnant when she died. We just wanted to find out who the father of the baby was."

"Well it wasn't me!" Tim Friar said adamantly. "Is that what you're suggesting?"

"No, no," Jessie said. "We ought to be going anyway." She got up and made a face at Bobby.

"She was just a little girl," Tim Friar carried on. "I've got children of my own. Why would I want to get involved with a little—" He stopped for a minute then said, "Wait, I remember now. Laurie and this bloke, they were getting out of a car. A dark blue hatchback I think, or it might have been black."

Laurie felt her legs go weak under her. Her dad had a dark blue Metro hatchback. Her dad was in Norwich for the half marathon. Her dad had grey hair and had admitted to her that Laurie had wanted him, that he had kissed her.

They went back out through the front of the

shop. The wind was pushing at the shutters of the shop. Across the road was a newsagent. On the stand outside was a billboard for the *Norfolk Times*. Underneath were the words, *KILLER GETS LIFE FOR MURDER OF GIRL 19*.

Jessie closed her eyes and felt the cold air chafe her skin. Bobby was behind her and was saying something but she couldn't hear and didn't want to.

Was her dad lying? She sat on the narrow single bed in the tiny attic room of the guest house. Had he come to Norwich to be with Laurie? She thought of him, doing his running shoes up, telling her about the short romance. She remembered his words. *I should've thrown the photo away really, but I was sort of touched. It shocked me out of mooning over Mum.*

She thought of Bobby's theories. That the mystery lover purposely fed Laurie with sleeping tablets and left her to die. She shook her head angrily even though there was no one in the room. Her dad, whose eyes misted over at the sad bits in films? Who was kind and forgiving – even now, she was sure, if her mum wanted to come back, he would take her.

He had kept the truth from her though. He had almost got involved with a seventeen-year-old girl and she would never have known if she hadn't found out for herself.

Then there was Bobby's other theory: that the man had made a suicide pact with Laurie and backed out of it at the last minute.

Jessie got up and paced the floor of the room. Was her dad capable of that? Her mum had left him after all those years of marriage and he hadn't tried to harm himself. It was impossible to imagine him sitting in the front of Laurie's car planning and executing such a ridiculous scheme. What would it have proved? If he were hiding the whole thing from her she would have found out anyway.

Jessie relaxed a little. She began to roll her head round on her shoulders.

What about her theory? That the man had rejected Laurie and that had driven her to suicide? Was her dad capable of that? She remembered his words again. *I was pretty horrible to her. I knew there was no point in letting her down gently. I just told her that she wasn't my type.*

There was a knock on her door.

"Jess, can I come in?" She heard Bobby's voice.

"Yes," she said. She wasn't going to find anything out by sitting around.

"Shall we go out and eat?"

"OK," she said and picked up her coat. As soon as she got home she'd talk to him about it again.

19

It was an Indian meal. They ate quietly, Jessie lost in her thoughts. A feeling of depression made it difficult to enjoy the food; on her plate she moved around the rice and bhaji and forked a couple of pieces of chicken tikka.

Bobby talked on and off.

"If it wasn't Tim Friar then it must be someone from London," he said and she nodded.

"An older bloke with a dark blue hatchback. A runner," he said and she swallowed a lump of nan bread.

"Dodger must know something," he said and fell silent for a few minutes.

Around them the music hummed and blended with the murmur of distant voices. The waitress was standing against the wall looking over at them. She seemed to be tapping the rhythm of a quite different tune on her leg. Her mouth was silently mouthing the words of some song. Jessie thought she looked familiar.

Bobby said, "Did I ever tell you about the time Dodger's mum rang me? When Dodger had that last big blow-up with her and the boyfriend?"

"No."

"It was odd really, that she should ring me, I mean. Dodger and me were never mates. I only knew him because of you and Laurie. Anyway, his mum rang. She was crying her eyes out, said they'd had a big row a few days before and Dodger hadn't been home since. She was in such a state that I went round there."

"His mum's flat?"

"Yes. She was so pleased to see me. She'd looked in an old address book of his. There were three numbers, Laurie's, yours and mine. She thought I'd be the best person to ring. She kept saying things like, 'I'm so glad Trevor's got good friends'. I didn't like to tell her that we were barely on speaking terms."

"What's she like, his mum?"

"Nice. Really nice. She's in her mid-thirties, had Dodger when she was a teenager. I saw her bloke too. About twenty-five. Good luck to her."

Jessie imagined an older woman with a younger

man. Then she thought of her dad, in his early forties and Laurie Drake, seventeen. The waitress came over and began to clear away the plates. Jessie knew her face but couldn't place her. As she walked away Bobby continued.

"They had this big row over tea one evening. She said that Dodger had been niggling at her boyfriend all day, making his smart ass comments. You know how irritating he could be."

Jessie bit her lip. She had never found Dodger irritating.

"The boyfriend – I forget his name – started to read an article in the paper about college school student suicides, you know those kids who are so wound up about their studies that they can't cope, and then he said, 'You had a friend, didn't you, who done herself in', or something like that.

"Dodger never said anything at first, ignored it. The boyfriend, though, started to recall the details and was chatting about it. He meant no offence – so Dodger's mum says – and he said, 'What was that they called it? A *Romeo and Juliet* suicide?' "

Jessie nodded. That was the detail that most people remembered.

"Apparently Dodger went berserk, pulled the table cloth off, smashed plates, made a run towards the boyfriend. It was sad really. His mum was crying when she told me, but what could I do?"

"And he never went back to live there?"

"I guess not. I did look for him. I told his mum I would. I didn't see him for weeks, but then one day he was just coming out of Murphy's as I was going in. I had a quiet word with him and told him I had talked to his mum."

"What did he say?"

"He told me to push off and mind my own business. So I did."

"Poor Dodger," Jessie said, thinking of him in his dishevelled clothes and his four-pack of lager.

"Thanks," said Bobby. "What about me?"

"But what's going to become of him?" she said, moving her hands off the table so the waitress could wipe the crumbs away.

Suddenly, Bobby said to the waitress, "Hello."

Jessie looked up at the girl. It was then that she recognized her. It was Tim Friar's daughter.

"You're the two that wanted to talk to my dad about Laurie Drake, aren't you?" The girl said it in a loud whisper, aggressively, as if the three of them were in the middle of an argument.

"Yes, we are," Jessie said, a little shaken.

"Well, let me tell you this," the girl leaned forward, across the table, making a show of straightening the tablecloth, "I used to work in the camp, casual, odd afternoons, and she made friends with me. Came round my house a couple of times, making out she wanted to see me but it was my dad she was after. You ask my mum. You ask my mum why she chucked my dad out of the house. Laurie Drake was no good. She was after anything in trousers. I was glad when I heard she died."

Then she leaned back and stood upright beside the table.

"Would you like a sweet, sir?" she said to Bobby. Jessie noticed her hands trembling.

Bobby's mouth was open.

"We'd like the bill," Jessie said. In her head she was thinking about her dad. If Laurie was linked with Tim Friar, then it meant her dad wasn't the man who was involved in her suicide. She stood up and a half moon smile radiated from her face.

"Certainly madam," the girl said and walked off.

20

They found Tim Friar in the third pub they went to. He was sitting at a table with three other men. When he saw them he tipped up his glass and finished his drink. He said a couple of things to the men and made his way towards them.

"I wondered if you two would be back," he said, walking past them, out of the door of the pub. They followed him outside, into the street. The wind had died down and the sky was navy blue with tiny stars. The moon was thin and looked like a smile in the sky. Tim Friar walked a few metres and came to the seafront. He leaned on the brick wall and looked down below. The waves were splashing lazily up the beach. They stood beside him and waited for him to say something. Jessie looked at Bobby and mouthed the words, "What now?", but he just shrugged his shoulders.

"Your little friend Laurie was a real teaser," Tim Friar said. "I liked her, most people did. She hung around with that lad, Trevor, but everyone could tell that there was nothing between them. She was always popping up places. In the canteen, in the offices, out on the playing field. 'Mr Friar,' she would say. 'Can I help you with the horse riding?' Or, 'Mr Friar, have you got any time to show me how to referee a game of basketball?' "

Jessie was trembling with cold and began to rub her hands together.

"She made friends with my daughter, Joanne. Then she was always in our house. In the kitchen having a cup of tea, in the living-room watching TV. I gave her a lift back to the site once or twice and she'd start these long conversations. Once she said that she couldn't get the passenger door open and I leaned across her to see why it was stuck. She stroked my arm." Tim Friar stopped and closed his eyes.

Bobby said, "Were you the father of her baby?"

"Lord no," Tim Friar said. "It never went that far. Not that I didn't want it to. But like I said, she was a tease."

"But why did your marriage break up if nothing happened?" Jessie said, using her hands to rub the sides of her arms.

"My wife is a proud woman. I took Laurie to the Norwich run, see. We were meant to spend the weekend together. I'd booked a room at a little guest house I knew. Everything was going well until this chap from London turned up. The one I told you about. That was it, I didn't see her no more. She was gone. I came back here after the race. Trouble was, I forgot to cancel the room and they rang. My wife answered. She's no fool, see. She knew what was supposed to happen."

"The man, in Norwich. Isn't there any more you can remember about him?" Bobby said.

"She asked me to leave, my wife did. I thought, it'll only be for a couple of weeks, till she gets over it. But it wasn't. She let our room to some painter. I thought it would only be for a couple of months, you know, until her pride had been soothed, until the whole town knew that I was crawling back on my hands and knees. But this painter, Bob his name is, he and her got on well and he's been there ever since."

Jessie tried to pull Tim Friar back on to the subject.

"You said this man, in Norwich, had a blue hatchback. Is there anything else you can remember?"

"Dark blue it was, not exactly a hatchback, more a sort of stationwagon, a French job, I think, Renault or Peugeot."

Jessie breathed deeply. Her dad had a Metro. He was out of the picture.

Tim Friar began to laugh gently.

"When I saw her back in camp, I said, 'You like your men a bit on the old side, don't you, young Laurie?' And she became all uppity. She said she preferred some mature men – get that, *some* mature men – because they were more intellectual. Let me see, what was it she said? Her boyfriend was an art lover. I said, 'All that thinking can make you soft.' She said, 'Oh, my man's not soft, he can go into the Welsh mountains in the middle of winter and survive for days.' Well, stuff him, I said."

Her dad had told her the truth, Jessie was sure. He wasn't linked to Laurie's death at all.

Amid her thoughts she noticed Tim Friar walking away.

"I'll be off now," he said. "Get one in before closing time."

They stood for a moment, Jessie's teeth chattering.

Bobby said, "Here, let me warm you up," and put his arm round her. They stood for a few minutes watching Tim Friar disappear up the road. Bobby finally said, "The more I hear about Laurie the more I realize how little I knew her."

"She just used everyone," Jessie said bitterly. She was thinking about Tim Friar and his broken marriage; then Dodger came into her head. Bobby's arm was heavy on her shoulder, his hand stroking her hair. The chill of the sea was penetrating her light jacket and she turned further into Bobby's shoulder.

He turned at the same time and leant down to kiss her. His mouth was warm but his face felt cold as it rubbed against hers. She kissed him back, her head turning to one side so that their lips fitted more comfortably. After what seemed like ages he stopped and she pulled back, the cold air making her wet lips feel chilled.

"I've been wanting to do that all day," he said. But she wasn't finished. She kissed him again, pushing her hands into his hair. All the tension of the evening dissolving, the words that Tim Friar had said circling in her head. She wanted to forget them, forget Laurie, start again, as though none of it had happened.

Tim Friar's wife had an artist living in her house; Laurie was a teaser; Laurie's man was an art lover; Mr Friar can you show me how to referee a basketball game?; intellectual men aren't soft; my man goes into the Welsh mountains for days and survives; he's an art lover.

The kissing stopped suddenly and Jessie felt that she had been shoved by an invisible hand.

Laurie's lover was a runner, who liked art and did survival training. He was from London.

"What's the matter, Jess?" Bobby said, his face red from the kissing.

"I know who it was! I know who Laurie's lover was!"

21

It was midday before they got back to London.
After stopping at Bobby's house to put their bags
down they started to walk towards the park.

"What if Lesley's there?" Bobby said.

"I don't know." Jessie shrugged her shoulders.

She pushed open the wrought-iron gate and
pressed the bell. The door opened a few seconds
later. Tom Bradley stood in the hall in his jeans and
T-shirt. He had no shoes on and his hair was wet,
as if he'd just got out of the shower.

"Hello," he said, smiling. "You've just missed
Lesley, I'm afraid. She's gone to the park with
the kids. She'll be about an hour, I should think."
He looked at his wrist but there was no watch
there.

"We haven't come to see Lesley," Jessie said. "We've come to see you. We know about you and Laurie Drake."

He stood for a moment staring first at Jessie then at Bobby. He opened his mouth to speak but nothing came out. Then his shoulders dropped and he exhaled. "You'd better come in," he said.

Tom Bradley sat at the long wooden table and told his story.

"It was when she used to baby-sit for us. I ran her home a couple of times. She knew I had an interest in art and she used to chat about paintings and artists. One night we talked for nearly an hour outside her house. Lesley was asleep when I got back, thank God."

He stopped and put his fingers over his mouth. His eyes were intent, staring down into the wood of the table, as if he was seeing something that they couldn't see.

"It was after that that it started. Just a couple of kisses, a hug before she got out of the car, a phone call, a lunch up in Epping Forest. I was very fond of her . . ."

Bobby's face was hardening and Jessie reached over and touched his hand.

"In the summer she was in Cromer and me and Lesley and the kids had a cottage in Sheringham, close by. I saw her at the Norwich half marathon and we arranged to spend a weekend together. Lesley didn't mind me going off to do some camping on my own. Laurie came with me. I knew then that it was getting too serious. She'd started to say things like, 'when you leave Lesley' and 'when we live together'."

"What did you say?" Jessie said.

"You're not going to tell Lesley anything about this are you? She'd be—"

"Why didn't you give her up?"

"I tried to. That time camping, I tried. She got into a real state. She started threatening me, saying things like, 'I'll commit suicide if you give me up, and then you'll be sorry.' I just tried to calm her down. I thought, if I played along for a while she'd get fed up, meet someone of her own age and go off with them."

"So you let it go on?"

"It was so easy," he said. "And she was so willing and sweet . . ."

"But what about your family?"

"Then she got pregnant. She did it on purpose you know."

Jessie looked away from him; he looked pathetic.

"You see, as soon as we got back from Cromer Lesley told me *she* was pregnant. I was distracted, I didn't know what to do."

Bobby got up and walked over to the photographs on the wall.

"So her suicide was very convenient then, for you and Lesley and the family, I mean."

"Yes, I suppose you could put it like that. Don't think I wasn't upset though. You're not going to tell Lesley any of this are you? She's innocent. It would hurt her enormously. Why should innocent people be hurt?"

"Wasn't Laurie an innocent person?" Bobby raised his voice.

"Yes. That's not what I meant."

"Did you have anything to do with her death?" Bobby said, sitting down across the table and looking straight at Tom Bradley.

"What do you mean?"

"You heard me."

"Her death? No, why on earth would you say that? The police said it was suicide."

"What if someone, with a lot to hide, tried to make it look like suicide? Someone who had a whole family to lose if Laurie chose to spill her secrets. Look at these . . ."

"Bobby . . ." Jessie said.

Bobby pulled the two anonymous notes out of his back pocket and flung them on the table. Tom Bradley read each one.

"Where did you get these?" he said.

"They were sent to me."

"But look, they don't suggest what you've just said at all. All it says is to find her lover. He is responsible for her death. I know. I know I'm responsible for her death. If she'd never got involved with me she'd still be alive now. But I never wanted her dead. Never. As if I could be some kind of murderer! Perhaps you want my alibi. Well ask your friend, that short kid."

"Dodger?" Jessie said.

"Trevor. He'll tell you I was here the whole evening when she died. I remember it like yesterday. How could I forget? Me and Lesley had just put the kids to bed and that young Trevor came round. I was all for telling him to go home but Lesley asked him to stay. All evening he sat with us. She tried talking to him but he just sat quietly, it seemed like hours. Then he said his mum had a new boyfriend and Lesley made him something to eat."

"Dodger was here that evening?" Jessie said, something niggling in the back of her mind.

"I drove him home about eleven. I remember he said something really odd about his mum. I said, 'I'm sorry you've fallen out with your mum, but once you get used to the idea, it'll be OK. You may even get to like this new man.' He said, 'There's years of difference between them. Anyway, it's me she should love, not him,' and he started to cry, there in the car. It was midnight before I got back home."

Tom Bradley stopped for a moment, lost in the

story. He looked at Jessie and Bobby. "So you see, I was with him from about eight until about midnight. You can ask him, you don't even have to mention it to Lesley."

It's me she should love, not him. There's years of difference.

Jessie could hear Dodger's words in her head. *You know, the night Laurie died I was down at Murphy's. Anyone will tell you that.*

He had lied to her. Had he forgotten where he was? Why had he thought he needed to give her an alibi anyway?

In the back of her head she could still hear Tom Bradley blustering quietly, "I cried the morning after she died. I made an oath never to be unfaithful, I've kept to it, I love my wife."

Then she remembered Dodger's friend, Billy, coming in with the newspapers. A pile of newspapers in the corner of the room, used perhaps for cutting letters and words out.

The sound of the front door opening stopped her thinking about it.

Tom Bradley came over to her and grabbed her hand.

"Please don't tell her," he said. "Laurie's dead now. Nothing can bring her back. Why destroy Lesley's life?"

Lesley Bradley wheeled a pushchair into the kitchen.

"Jessie and Bobby. What a surprise. How are you? Have you come to see me?"

She stopped and looked around the room at the three of them standing there. The toddler ran over to Tom Bradley saying, "Daddy, we see'd some big ducks."

"Is something wrong?" Lesley said, undoing the straps on the pushchair and pulling the baby out of it. The six-month-old baby. The same age as Laurie's would have been.

"No," Jessie said, walking over to Bobby and taking his arm. "No, we haven't got time now I'm afraid. We'll call and have a chat another day."

"OK." Lesley looked puzzled.

As they were closing the door, Jessie could hear her walking back up the long hallway calling, "Tom! Tom!"

"Let him sort it out," Jessie said and they walked off to the park.

"But why should Dodger send me anonymous notes about Laurie's death? Why would he do that?"

"I don't know. I don't know!" Jessie said with frustration. They sat back against a wall and watched a gardener pull dead plants from a bed. None of it was making any sense. "Let's go back to the beginning. The note."

Bobby started to recite, "Remember what Juliet

says. Farewell. God knows when we shall meet again. I love you, Laurie."

"We know that Laurie wasn't religious, so she couldn't have been talking about meeting in some afterlife."

"But that's exactly it. Romeo and Juliet did die together, that's why I thought that it might have been a planned double suicide that went wrong."

"No, they didn't."

"What?"

"They didn't die together. Remember, Juliet never meant to die. She took the drug from Friar Laurence that would make her look dead. She was meant to wake up so that Romeo could come and collect her and they could live happily ever after. What if Laurie took the drugs, meaning to wake up later, you know, a fake attempt, to gain sympathy? That would explain the note and the troll."

"No, we've already been through that. If that was the case then why park right out of the way, in a spot where no one could possibly find her?"

"It works though! If Laurie had been found half dead, then Tom Bradley would have had to do something. It would certainly have broken his marriage up. In the end Laurie probably thought that he would come to her."

"Then why not take fewer drugs? The police said she took a dozen or more tablets."

"Because she wanted it to look as though she meant it. To frighten him into doing something."

"It would have killed the baby."

"But she wasn't really interested in the baby. It was Tom Bradley she wanted. Don't you see? Juliet planned her death. Friar Laurence was meant to go and wake her up and take her to Romeo. What if Laurie planned it in the same way? What if someone was supposed to make sure that she woke up?"

"A Friar Laurence figure?"

"Yes."

Jessie got up from the wall.

"I think we ought to go and see Dodger."

22

The community centre was deserted. Jessie called out for Dodger but there was no answer. She took Bobby in by the back way. There was no sign of Billy either.

They went into the room that Jessie had been in before. Everything was the same, only the newspapers looked as though they'd been ruffled. She walked across to the desk and opened the top one. There were spaces where words had been cut out. The pages looked grey in the dim light.

"*This* is where he lives?" Bobby said, visibly shocked.

"Look, these are the newspapers he used." Jessie picked one of them up. Bobby walked across and looked at the contents on the table.

"But why would Dodger send anonymous notes? I don't understand," he said, shrugging his shoulders.

A voice from behind said, "You never did understand very much though, did you, Bobby?"

Jessie and Bobby turned round. Dodger was standing there.

"Dodge." Bobby nodded curtly.

"The lovely Jessie as well. Have you finished playing Sherlock Holmes and Watson? Have you worked out the great mystery?" Dodger walked across to the table. Jessie could smell alcohol and dried sweat. For a moment she felt a wave of nausea. Dodger took something out of his pocket and dropped it on to the table. It was a Stanley knife. Jessie felt Bobby's hand grip her elbow.

"Why did you send the notes, Dodge?" he said, his voice unsteady.

"To get you going. To get you started." Dodger said the words loudly, as if he were talking to a small child. "God!" He walked across to the boarded-over window and bent down to look out of one of the small cracks. "It must have been as plain as the nose on your face that something was wrong with her death. Didn't you care?" He turned round and looked straight at them. In the semi darkness Jessie couldn't work out what expression Dodger had on his face. He could have been smiling, although his voice was hard and unwavering.

"But everyone said it was suicide, Dodge." She said the words softly, persuasively.

He mimicked her though. "Everyone said it was suicide, Dodge."

He walked back over to the table and picked up the Stanley knife. He fiddled with it for a moment until the blade slid out. He used it to dig at the table while he talked.

"Maybe it was suicide, but someone made her do it. She was involved with someone, some older bloke. It's his fault. I don't suppose, in all your pathetic detective work you've managed to find out who it was?"

"It was Tom Bradley." Bobby said the words. Jessie turned and looked at him in astonishment. Surely he could see that Dodger was unhinged?

"Tom Bradley." Dodger stopped scraping the table and whispered the words. He looked around the room. "Tom Bradley," he said again, slowly, almost relishing the sound of the name.

"But he had nothing to do with her death, Dodge. You must know that! You were with him the night she died."

"But he made her do it! Don't you see? If she'd never been involved with him, she'd be here now. She'd be walking around the streets, shopping, going to the cinema, getting a job or at university. She'd be alive. If she hadn't met him!"

"But she wouldn't be with you, Dodge. She

wouldn't be your girlfriend," Bobby said, nastiness in his voice.

"Nor yours." Dodger pushed the knife into the table so that it stood up by itself. "I must go. I've got someone to see." He said it distractedly. Then he leant back against the table and began to talk. Jessie felt Bobby's hand pulling her gently. After a few seconds she realized that he was moving, imperceptibly towards the door.

"I was in love with her. She knew that. She was nice to me sometimes, sometimes she just treated me like dirt. I hadn't seen her for a few days and she rang me and asked me to go round there. She wanted me to do her a favour. I was dead pleased, you know I got all dressed up. I went to see her. It was the day before she died.

"I thought that she might have finished with him. I thought there might be a chance for me, but she was still on about how wonderful he was. Then she told me what she planned to do.

"She wanted me to get her some downers. She was going to drive right into the forest where there could be no chance of anyone finding her. She was going to take the lot at about eight o'clock. Then—"

Dodger stopped. In the distance Jessie could hear the whine of a siren. Bobby edged them a couple of steps towards the door and Dodger looked around confused, his story broken by the noise of the police car. He looked at Bobby and Jessie with a puzzled expression as if he didn't really understand why they were there.

"Have you told the police?" he said. He pulled the Stanley knife out of the table and began cutting into the wood again.

"No," Jessie said, wishing that she had.

"The police did nothing!" he said, leaning back again, the noise of the siren fading into the distance. "They're not interested in responsibility. They don't care about whose fault it was."

"Whose fault was it though?" Bobby said. Jessie turned round to give him a warning look. It wasn't worth riling Dodger when he was clearly so unstable. Jessie looked at the Stanley knife, gouging chunks out of the table.

"Bradley's. You've just said, haven't you?"

"Wasn't it yours?" Bobby continued, taking a step away from Jessie towards Dodger. "You said she told you what she planned. It wasn't just that, was it? She involved you! You were part of the plan. You were meant to stop her. She probably told you exactly which bit of the forest she'd be in and you were meant to ring the police. She probably even told you what time to do it. And you let her die."

Dodger said nothing but his breathing became shallow, and Jessie watched him as he took the knife and slid the blade back and put it in his pocket. He was calm although Bobby was trembling and she was stiff with tension.

"I've got to go," he said and he took a step towards the door. Jessie put her hand on Bobby's arm. If he could just let him go, then they could ring the police. It wasn't worth getting into a row with Dodger.

"You killed her. It was *your* fault. You were meant to stop her and you didn't!" Bobby screamed the last words and then lunged at Dodger. They both toppled to the floor and Jessie found herself looking at a tangle of arms and legs.

"Stop . . . don't," she said, but they continued to roll towards the table, then away close to the wall. Bobby seemed to be on top of Dodger most of the time; Jessie could only see the back of his head and his shoulders straining to hold Dodger's small frame on the floor. She could see Dodger's face as well, his teeth clenched, his eyes swivelling wildly. He looked as though he was trying to lift a great weight.

Between breaths, Bobby was saying, "It's your fault, no one else's . . ."

The door opened suddenly and Dodger's friend, Billy, stood there.

"Trev," he said. Bobby looked round and in that moment lost his hold. Dodger seemed to sit up off the floor, his great shoulders and arms gripping Bobby and pushing him backwards so that he fell towards the table leg.

"Bobby . . ." Jessie said helplessly as she heard the thud of his head hitting the table leg.

He didn't answer though, and as Dodger scrambled out from under him his body slumped to the side, his eyes closed, his mouth slightly open, half his face seemingly glued to the floor.

"My God, what have you done?" Jessie said, kneeling down.

Dodger looked at Bobby for a moment and then stood up straight, using his hand to dust himself off.

"It's time to go." Dodger said it in a booming voice although Jessie could see his hand trembling. "Time to see Tom Bradley," he added, pushing his hand deep into his pocket and taking out the Stanley knife.

"Bobby needs an ambulance!" Jessie said.

"Au revoir," Dodger said and walked out of the door with Billy. When the door was shut Jessie heard the click of the key turning in the lock. She shook Bobby's shoulder in desperation and then noticed the thin line of blood that was seeping from his head onto the floor.

23

Jessie pulled at the boards that were across the windows, but it was all show. They were solid, old floorboards that had been nailed to the window frame with what seemed like six-inch nails.

She stood back, defeated. Bobby was still lying on the floor, unconscious. Dodger was on his way to Tom Bradley's with a knife in his pocket.

She leant against the desk and thought it through. The door was locked; the windows boarded up; yet she had to get out and get to a phone. By her feet was Bobby's inert body, the trickle of blood looking dark brown in the dim light.

In films there was always a crowbar or a screwdriver which could be used to dig away at the lock.

But all that was left in the room were the old sleeping-bags and the Primus stove and tin kettle. The cassette player was gone. There was a pile of dusty newspapers on the table.

It was hopeless. She had no tool or weapon with which she could try to get them out. In the back of her head there was a tune playing quietly. She bent down to look at Bobby. His eyes were still closed and for some reason she put her hand across his forehead to see if he was hot. The tune in her head was getting louder and she used both of her hands to rub furiously at her scalp. How could she have music in her head at a time like this?

It didn't go away though. It was there, guitars, drums, a saxophone and some voices. She stood up, her muscles tensing; it was outside. The music was coming from outside the community centre. She stepped across to the window and looked out of one of the gaps in the wood. Across the street, some hundred or so metres away, were a boy and a girl, standing together. By their side, on the ground, was a cassette player.

Jessie shouted, "Hey, help!" But it was weak and neither the boy nor the girl looked over.

She took a deeper breath and shouted, "Help! Help! Help!" But the couple were kissing and engrossed with each other.

In the end she stood very still, took a deep breath in and shouted, at the top of her voice,

"HELP! HELP! HELP! HELP!" Then she gasped for breath, leaning against the wall, her heart pounding against her rib cage.

The boy stopped, looked up, turned in her direction, then looked back at the girl. He bent down to pick up the cassette player and Jessie realized that they were going to walk away. She took as much breath into her lungs as she could and screamed, "HELPHELPHELPHELPHELPHELP . . ."

And both of the young people looked round. Unable to speak, she pushed her fingers out of the cracks between the wood. She felt the burning in her throat from where she had forced every last decibel of her voice to spill out.

When they got to the window she croaked, "My friend's hurt and the door's locked. Please open it and get an ambulance."

The girl ran in one direction and the boy disappeared from view. After a minute or so she heard the click of the key.

So Dodger had left it in the lock! She shook her head.

"What's happened?" the boy said, looking from Bobby to her then back to Bobby again.

"Too much to explain," Jessie said, grabbing the boy's arm, wanting to hug him. "Tell the police to go to 22 Rosemary Avenue. Quick. I'll see them there. Tell them it's about Laurie Drake."

And she ran from the room, leaving Bobby on the floor and the boy looking at him in astonishment.

24

The front door was open when she got to the Bradleys' house. She had to stand still for a few seconds though, taking breath in slowly, recovering from the run that she had just done. She'd been lucky: being Sunday, there was little traffic and she'd sprinted and run, crossing roads without looking, thinking ahead to the next street and the next short cut.

When she got to the park she had run herself out and had to take giant steps instead, looking ahead all of the time, thinking about Dodger and his Stanley knife and his hatred for Tom Bradley.

A few metres away from the house was Billy, Dodger's friend, leaning against a car, his eyes heavy lidded, not even seeming to notice her.

When she got her breath back she crept into the hallway. The house was silent except for Lesley Bradley's voice. It was coming from the kitchen.

"Suppose what you say is true Trevor – and I don't believe it for a minute – suppose Laurie had been involved with Tom, what good would it do if you hurt him? It's not going to bring Laurie back."

Jessie stepped closer. Her old tutor's voice sounded calm and reasonable. It was probably something she'd learned on a counselling course. She pushed the door open a crack and looked in.

Dodger had his back to her. He was standing by the chair that Tom Bradley was sitting in. Jessie couldn't see very clearly but he had something in his hand.

Lesley was sitting opposite with the toddler on her lap. Jessie couldn't see if the other child was in the room. She heard Dodger's voice.

"If it wasn't for him Laurie would still be alive." Dodger stretched his arms up in the air. In one hand he had the Stanley knife. Then he put his arm round Tom Bradley's neck. "You had your fun with my Laurie. You didn't care about anyone. She said that you loved her, that you were going to leave your wife for her."

Jessie could see Lesley Bradley's face flinch at this. The toddler on her lap was beginning to struggle, saying "Mum, Mum, Mum."

Dodger took his arm from Tom's neck and

moved away slightly. His feet were moving clumsily, in an unco-ordinated way. The knife was swaying in his hand, the tiny blade menacing. She felt a mounting panic in her chest. Dodger was full of anger; he could do anything.

Jessie took a deep breath and opened the door. Before Dodger could turn round to see who it was she had stepped across and, with all the strength she had left, pushed him forward so that he fell across the table, the Stanley knife dropping from his hand, spinning and falling onto the floor. Tom Bradley moved quickly and put his foot on it.

Lesley Bradley stood up, her mouth open with shock. Dodger lay, face down on the table, where he had landed.

Then he began to cry.

His back moved up and down with great sobs and with his hands he covered the sides of his face so that he couldn't be seen.

Lesley walked across to her husband and handed the toddler to him. In a tight voice she said, "Take her upstairs, out of the way."

"It's not true," Tom Bradley said. "None of it."

"Just get out of my sight," Lesley said and watched him with a stony expression as he turned and walked out of the door.

Dodger lay across the table and Lesley walked

round and sat in the chair nearest to him. She pulled one of his hands off his face, held it tightly and said, "Tell me what happened."

Jessie leant against the wall, facing the photos of Tom the runner, Tom the survival expert. Dodger began to talk.

"I got the tablets off a mate I knew down at the pool hall. I took them to her on the Saturday afternoon. She was excited. She had that lucky toy of hers, that plastic thing with the pink hair. She took the tablets and put them in the tiny rucksack. It was like she was saving sweets for herself. She told me where she was going to drive to. She told me what time she was going to take the tablets. Eight o'clock. Give them a couple of hours to work she said then ring up the police. Say you were just passing with a woman friend and you saw this girl asleep in a car. Say you don't want to leave your name. Just make sure you tell them which car and exactly where it is. It's simple she said, easy as pie."

"But you didn't do it, did you Dodger?" Jessie said, her voice faint. In her head she held an imaginary picture of Laurie, confident that Dodger would keep his end of the bargain, going to sleep in the front seat of her battered mini. Maybe she saw herself as Juliet. Maybe, as she was dropping into that final sleep, she was planning her days with Tom Bradley.

Now she was dead, packed in a wooden box under the ground.

Lesley Bradley was still holding Dodger's hand.

"You didn't ring the police. You came round here instead. You let her die." Jessie spat the words out, and Dodger began to cry again. Then, afraid that she was going to cry too, she turned and walked out of the room. She passed Tom Bradley on her way out. As she got outside into the street a police car was pulling up. WPC Williams got out of the passenger seat and walked up to her.

"Inside," was all Jessie could say. She looked round to see Tom Bradley's face, his jaw hanging open, his eyes darting here and there.

They could explain. She had had enough. She pulled herself together.

"Has Bobby, the injured boy, been taken to the hospital?" she asked another policeman who was fiddling with his car radio.

"The King George, about ten minutes ago," he said.

Jessie began to walk up the street. She passed Billy who was gazing vacantly at the commotion.

Bobby was in hospital. She would go and see him. Now that Laurie Drake was really dead and buried they could sort things out.

There was a determination in her step as she walked along and without knowing why, she began to think about the university place that was waiting for her the next year. In the distance she saw a bus that was going by the hospital. She waved it down and got on.

Anne Cassidy

Anne Cassidy has been writing for about five years. She is a keen reader of detective stories and thrillers, and her favourite writers are Sue Grafton, Patricia Cornwell and Ruth Rendell.

As well as *Driven to Death*, she also has two other novels, *Big Girls' Shoes* and *In Real Life* in print, both stories with a central mystery that has to be worked out. She also writes for younger children.

She is a part-time teacher and lives in London with her husband and son.

Coming soon in the Point Crime *series* . . .

Final Cut
David Belbin

They were in the final week of filming and Leo Fitzgerald was precisely on schedule. So far, all of the film had been shot on location. Even the wedding had taken place in Bradlington Hall. But the scene they were shooting today could only be done in the studio. Leo had hired Shepherd's Gate, an old studio on the edge of London, an hour's drive from Bradlington. Jon gathered that the director had got a cheap deal, because the studio was about to be shut down and demolished. They didn't need insurance cover, either.

The sound stage was shabby and decrepit. As the crew had prepared it over the weekend, they sneezed endlessly from the dust which was settled everywhere. But now it was relatively clean and ready to be set on fire. Mary, the extra who had been Jon's date at the ballroom scene, three weeks before, had landed a speaking part as Jane, an old friend of Melissa's. Now the two of them were sitting in a replica of Melissa's room at Bradlington Hall. This scene was taking place just before the wedding, as Jane helped Melissa into her wedding dress.

"You look gorgeous," Jane said. "I'm so happy for you."

"Thanks for agreeing to be a bridesmaid at such short notice," Melissa told her. "You saved my life."

"Believe me," Jane said, "I wouldn't have missed this for anything."

Then she paused, noticing the tear which was dripping down onto Melissa's white dress.

"Melissa, what is it? What's wrong?"

Melissa turned her tear-stained eyes to Jane. "I can't get it out of my mind. Suppose Aidan's been telling the truth? Suppose Matthew did murder all of his other wives? Suppose I'm next?"

Jane gave her a hug, then handed her a tissue.

"You know you're being silly," she said. "Matthew's been unlucky, but all three of his wives died in accidents. They weren't murdered. And Aidan's been psychologically disturbed since he was a child. Matthew showed you the doctor's reports. That's why he didn't invite him to the wedding, in case he does something crazy."

"But maybe Aidan's right," Melissa protested. "Maybe I'm the one acting crazy, marrying someone thirty years older than me."

"Either you love him or you don't," Jane told her. "Age doesn't come into it."

Jon watched the monitor as the camera closed in on Sarah's face, showing the doubt in her eyes. How could anyone say that she couldn't act?

"Cut!" Leo Fitzgerald called. "OK, that's a wrap. Let's get on with setting up the fire scene."

Jon hurried into action. This was the most complicated set-up in the film. Minutes after Melissa and Matthew exchanged vows, his sister would be trapped in her room when the building catches fire. All of the other guests get out. Then Aidan, after an argument with Matthew, would charge back into the building and save her life.

"Now do you believe me?" he would ask, once they were outside. But Melissa would still be uncertain, knowing that someone set the fire up, but not knowing whether it was the father or the son.

The actual wedding scene had been shot weeks earlier at the stately home. To keep location costs to a minimum, Fitzgerald arranged that the couple marry in the mansion's chapel, then have the reception in the house. The set had been decorated to look like the house they were supposed to be in. Carpenters had built a mock-up of the west wing. Beyond Sarah's room were two corridors and a staircase. The shots of guests watching the fire from outside would be faked later, using visual overlays during the editing.

The trick with fire scenes, Leo Fitzgerald explained to the crew, was not to burn the actual sets, but to burn the plastic gunk which they had spread over all of the walls. Timing was crucial. If the first take went wrong, you were left with scorched walls.

Two special effects people would have to put out the fires, repaint the walls, then wait for the paint to dry before spreading the flammable gunk all over them again. But the crew only had a day to shoot the whole thing, and it was already getting on for noon.

"We're going for everything in one take," Fitzgerald announced over the tannoy. "Everybody into position."

Sarah sat in the part of the set which was her dressing room looking calm. Mary, the extra who had landed the part of the bridesmaid, was on the edge of the set. She had a short scene with Luke Kelly, who was going to go into the fire himself. Fitzgerald had offered Kelly a stuntman double, but Luke wouldn't hear of it.

Jon got onto the crane which was holding the camera for the overhead shots. He had been promoted the previous day, to Camera Assistant, when the woman whose job it was had come down with appendicitis. Now he would have a dual credit on the film, and he'd be able to tell people precisely which scenes he'd helped to shoot. He was responsible for the safety of the camera and maintaining the level of film stock. He was tired, having stayed up late the night before, reading the manual, then arriving early this morning to make sure he was fully confident with the equipment.

As the crane lifted into the air, Jon saw Slacker,

wearing technician's overalls, standing by a row of fire extinguishers. The youth must have talked his way into a job on the safety crew. Sarah had insisted on maximum safety for this scene and Leo had assured her that there was no risk. Near Slacker, Brett was getting into his position on one of the corridor sets. Who started the fire? Brett or Luke? No one knew. Fitzgerald still hadn't revealed how he intended to end the film. Jon wondered whether the director had even made his own mind up yet.

Sarah waited patiently for the scene to begin. This was her most complicated scene, but she didn't have to learn any lines for it. Mainly she had to react – to the smoke coming in through the door, to the flames surrounding her in the corridor. She had to look out of a window and consider whether to jump. Luke, meanwhile, would fight his way through the flames and carry her to safety, just as she seemed about to be overcome by the smoke.

Luke's part in the film was nearly over. He had to leave a week before the end of the shoot in order to start work on another film, *Cool College 5*, which he wasn't looking forward to.

"Why don't you join me?" He'd said to her last night, "as soon as this shoot is over. You could fly to L.A., stay at my house in the valley. We'd have a great time."

"You'd be working," she protested.

"No one works that hard in L.A. Making movies there isn't like it is here, with a slave-driver director. It's laid back."

"I'll think about it," Sarah told him, cautiously. "I do have some other assignments lined up. I'd have to talk to my agent."

"You don't want to carry on as a model after this," Luke insisted. "Come to L.A. with me. Stay as long as you like. I'll introduce you to people. You'll get lots of offers, I promise."

Sarah made no promises in return. Last night, Luke told her that he loved her, but Sarah didn't tell him that she loved him back, even though she did, with all her heart. She was too frightened of getting hurt.

"Sarah, are you ready?" The assistant director asked. "You look a million miles away."

"I'm ready."

As soon as Sarah got into position, the walls were set alight. Helped by a fan, smoke began to seep beneath the door in the room where Sarah sat. The crew filmed Sarah's reaction shots quickly. Then, when the flames had built up enough, the camera moved in to a medium close-up of her opening the door, seeing the flames, and being driven back by the heat.

The heat from the flames was real. It shocked Sarah. Never mind Luke being offered a stunt double, maybe she should have one for herself. Sarah went to the window, opened it, and screamed for help. The actual sound of the scream didn't matter, as it would be re-dubbed later. She backed into the room. Now all she had to wait for was Luke, coming to rescue her.

Off stage, Sarah heard Luke being given his instruction to get into position. He had a conflict with Brett first of all, which ended with Aidan knocking his father out in the middle of the flames. Sarah could barely make out their dialogue above the sound of the fire. It was hard to believe that the plastic stuff they'd been spreading on the walls could make so much noise. The fire was so realistic. Flames were even beginning to lick their way across the front of the sound stage. No one had told Sarah that this was going to happen. Unless . . . Sarah backed up against the wall . . . suppose it was going wrong? But no, she was an actress. There was a camera crew only yards away from her. She mustn't panic, mustn't spoil the take, or it would be hours before they could start again.

From above, Jon could see that the fire was getting out of control. Fitzgerald kept on filming regardless. Sarah wasn't in any danger, but the fire in the corridors was way too strong – the actual sets were on fire and smoke was building up. Still, the camera kept rolling. Sarah continued to act, despite the fact that, at the edge of the set, Luke had walked off and was arguing with the director.

"I can't go through that! It's too hot!"

"Don't be a wimp," Fitzgerald told him. "Now! Go!"

Luke moved back into camera shot. Brett was still lying on the floor where Luke had knocked him out earlier. In a moment, he would be able to get up, as the camera followed Luke across the set. But when the camera followed Luke, Brett didn't get up. The smoke must have got to him. And the fire was dangerously near – not just to Brett – flames were building up around the whole stage now. It was becoming an inferno. In her room at the side of the set, sweat poured down Sarah's wedding dress. Meanwhile, Luke was trying to make his way across the set. He climbed a burning staircase. Then he crossed the first corridor, starting as he burnt his arm by brushing it against a wall.

It was impossible to see what was going on in the final corridor. Smoke billowed through, flooding the room where Sarah waited.

"This is ridiculous," Jon shouted into the intercom. "Luke and Sarah are in danger! Get them out!"

But the little red light on the intercom didn't come on and Jon realized that the electrics were probably out, too. If this went on much longer, the entire studio would be ablaze. . . .